A HIGHWAYMAN'S MAIL ORDER BRIDE

WESTWARD HEARTS

BLYTHE CARVER

A HIGHWAYMAN'S MAIL ORDER BRIDE

The last thing a mail order bride needs is a highwayman's intervention in the form of a stagecoach robbery. Especially when time is of the essence and she needs a father for her baby. Preferably before she begins to show.

When Melissa married John Carter because her family couldn't afford to feed her, she had no idea of the cruelty of the man. John Carter beats her mercilessly and makes her life a living hell.

After seeing an ad in the paper for paid passage westward, she answers the ad in the hopes to use the ticket to escape John Carter.

She gets on a coach from Boston, heading west, with no money, and needing a roof over her head. Not just for herself, but for the baby she's carrying, a baby she has to save from John Carter's cruelty. Expecting a baby has changed the stakes for Melissa. She must provide a safe and loving home for the child. Time is of the essence if she is to marry in time to convince her new husband that the baby she'll give birth to is his.

A stagecoach robbery is a deterrent she did not count on, nor need. When the robbers learn her husband is a wealthy rancher, she's taken hostage, costing her precious time in a plan that hinges on timeliness.

She hates the leader of the highwaymen. Hates him with a passion and is beyond angry that the time is ticking while he negotiates her ransom.

Jed Cunningham's a highwayman, certainly, but one with honor. And a heart, it seems. He can't stand the idea of sending the stunning feisty Melissa Carter to marry a rich rancher. She's precisely the kind of woman who needs to be loved.

But she doesn't seem to see that.

1

The coach jolted and bounced over the rough road, drawing a groan from the passengers aboard it as they fought to remain in their seats. How were the rules of polite society to be maintained when a person all but landed in the lap of another every time the stagecoach hit a bit of uneven ground?

And it seemed as though that was all they'd come across since their most recent stop, to the point where several of the men onboard questioned whether they traveled a dedicated road at all. The Butterfield line was known for its speed, everyone knew that, but the men currently struggling against nausea and sore backsides—it truly did wear on the body, bouncing up and down as they did— questioned if that speed was the result of cutting across the open prairie.

Only one passenger of the nine aboard did not complain or even open their mouth except to cough into a handkerchief when the dust from the wheels became too much to bear.

She happened to be the only woman on board, as well.

While the journey was a difficult one, especially since she'd made the change from the smaller, slower-moving but far less taxing stagecoach lines of the east, she minded little so long as she got where she was going, and in a hurry.

Between Boston and St. Louis, they had taken long meal breaks in reputable inns and boarding houses. She'd been able to wash away the dust and grime, as well, and had even felt downright refreshed upon climbing back into the stagecoach after each stop.

Now?

The situation had changed, to say the least.

It mattered not to Melissa Carter, who pressed herself into the rear corner of the coach and did what she could to be forgettable.

An old trick, one she'd mastered over many years. Disappearing. Fading into the background. Avoiding notice at all costs.

Even so, there was no avoiding the glances. The curious stares she noted through lowered lashes, while the men in the coach believed her to be asleep. The deferential treatment whenever the opportunity arose—a hand into and out of the coach, a place at the head of the line while awaiting food. They made certain she was served first and even watched their language when conversing over the meager suppers provided at the ramshackle establishments which marked each leg of their progress.

There was little conversation in the coach, as the need to shout over pounding hooves and creaking wheels made it all but impossible to hear the person seated just beside or in front of oneself. To say nothing of the choking dust which constantly stirred in the air.

One did what one could to avoid breathing it in, which left the art of conversation severely lacking.

Melissa adjusted herself as primly as possible, wishing she could stretch her legs rather than propping them atop a sack of mail, always careful to avoid brushing against the leg of the man beside her. A kindly man, or so he appeared. Older, with thick, white whiskers and a shy smile. The smile of a man unaccustomed to a woman's presence.

She wondered idly as to his destination. Mr. Hawkins, seated in front and facing the two rear benches, was in banking and made a habit of checking his gold pocket watch every twenty minutes or so. Mr. Lang was headed west to inquire about purchasing a tract of land adjacent to the new railroad everyone seemed to be excited over—he had even convinced Mr. Greenley, a scarred war veteran visiting his sister in San Francisco, that land prices would soon skyrocket.

"Now is the time to invest," he'd advised all of the men at the table one night while they took their supper, gesturing with his spoon between bites of baked beans. "With the railroad completed and the two halves connected, you'll see. There will be a commercial boon such as the country has never experienced."

One of the men had cleared his throat then, shifting his

eyes to where Melissa sat at one corner of the long table with her head slightly lowered as she ate. But she'd been watching, always aware of her surroundings, and Mr. Lang had all but blushed as he apologized for discussing business matters in such exuberant tones while there was a lady present.

Melissa never could understand this, but she'd kept her opinions to herself. It was better to smile and nod, to be demure and silent.

All the better for the men to forget she'd ever existed.

For this was not a pleasure trip. She was not visiting a sister in California, nor was she settling the estate of a client as Mr. Dearborn—a lawyer—was. She was not purchasing land. She was not overseeing the opening of a new bank.

She was getting married.

The thought of Mr. Mark Furnish and their upcoming wedding made her clutch her reticule tighter than ever. The plain little drawstring bag held the two letters Mr. Furnish had sent her over the course of their short correspondence—one thick letter telling her of himself and of his ranch which sat a two-hour ride from Carson City, Nevada, and the other, shorter letter which came with the tickets for the stagecoach.

He had taken pains to tell her of the hardship such a life could be for a woman—one thing she had appreciated about the man, other than the promise of marriage and a life away from Boston—was his honesty. He had few neighbors, he'd warned, and life for a woman could be quite lonely, especially when work on the ranch required him to be away from the house for days at a stretch.

Melissa had assured him she was more than pleased to accept this, and she had not told a lie. For being left alone for days at a stretch sounded pretty much akin to heaven in her estimation.

Of all the things she'd never had, privacy was the one she'd most longed for.

That, and love, but privacy had always felt like the more attainable of the two.

The stagecoach lurched, sending the elbow of the kindly old gentleman to her right squarely into her ribs. "Oh, I'm terribly sorry," he stammered, the cheeks above his whiskers going pink.

She favored him with the same smile she gave all the men and merely shook her head.

"It was nothing," she murmured, hoping to reassure him.

The truth of the matter was, she felt little through her whalebone stays, but a man would not understand that without explanation, and she was not about to explain the finer points of female undergarments to a stranger.

Though the thought of doing so brought a wicked smile to her lips which she was quick to cover with her handkerchief. How much redder the man's cheeks would burn!

That flash of wickedness was a sign of the freedom she already sensed, even though she had yet to reach her destination, and in fact would likely not do so for another week, or even two. She had lost track of the days.

When she realized this and remembered how vital it was that she reach Carson City and marry the rancher she'd never seen, anxiety twisted itself in her belly. Would that the horses would put on greater speed, though her sharp intellect told her there was no chance of them making better time.

As it was, the coach moved nearly through the entire day and night, stopping no more than a few hours at the last stage so the driver might fetch a bit of sleep. This, she'd learned from Mr. Lang's pocket watch, was normally between the hours of two and five o'clock in the morning.

Otherwise, the stagecoach rolled on.

They'd been blessed with dry weather since leaving St. Louis, though even in her urgent haste to reach Carson City, Melissa wished for at least one rainfall. Something to settle the dust which left her scalp itching beneath her simple straw bonnet.

There was no removing the thing, as she'd learned after the first day of travel. By the time they'd made their final stop that evening, her honey blonde hair had turned the brown color of a field mouse. She'd hardly recognized herself in the looking glass.

"We ought to be stopping for breakfast soon," Mr. Greenley announced, peering out the small, square window in the coach's door. "It looks like midmorning."

Breakfast. Her stomach turned at the thought of it. While the meager selection they'd been afforded up to that point was not below her standards—she had eaten far worse than baked beans with a bit of salt pork, old potatoes, and stale cornbread—she could rarely bear the thought of eating in the morning.

A new development.

One of many she would face over the course of the next months—by her calculation, almost exactly eight-and-one-half.

It would not be much longer before her intended would refuse to accept his having fathered the child growing in her belly. She hoped he was as ill-advised as to the nature of such processes as most men, and that the prospect of a child—perhaps a son who would one day take ownership of the Furnish Ranch and its fifty-thousand acres—would blind him to simple mathematics.

Which was why speed was of the essence. Speed and a quick wedding ceremony upon reaching Carson City. She did not care even to wait until they reached the ranch. So long as he bedded her that night.

They rolled to a stop, the driver shouting instructions to the boys who ran for the coach upon its arrival. There was mail to be fetched from inside, which Melissa knew from recent experience would merely be replaced by another sack or more. Soon, there would be nowhere for them to sit at all, the entirety of the coach's interior replaced by great canvas bags.

The stillness and silence which replaced so much loud motion caused everyone in the coach, even Melissa, to laugh. When the men spoke as they climbed over the mail sacks and out the door, they shouted out of habit when a murmur would do just as well.

"Mrs. Furnish?" Mr. Lang offered his hand to help her alight from the coach, as always. The perfect gentleman.

Neither he nor any of the men present—including the driver and his shotgun-toting partner—needed to know the truth. That she was not yet wedded to the Nevada rancher who she'd found through an ad he placed in the newspaper, seeking a bride.

She extended her left hand, the gold of her wedding band flashing in the sun.

A wedding band placed upon her finger during a marriage ceremony, not by Mark Furnish but by another man whose face she hoped to never see again except in the nightmares she feared she'd always suffer. Painful nightmares, memories of his fists and the cruel words he'd screamed in her face too many times to count.

Her traveling companions did not need to know that her true, married name was Melissa Carter, either. Mrs. John Carter, of Boston, Massachusetts.

A woman whose husband would likely beat her close to death and perhaps kill their unborn child if he knew what she'd done.

2

Z eke stretched out on his back, elbows propping him up, his worn-out boots crossed at the ankle. "When's it gonna rain?" he groaned.

A familiar complaint, one which all of the men shared when the air became dry as a bone and the dust kicked up in funnel clouds all across the plains.

"Dry heat's better than wet heat," Jed reminded him.

"I don't know about that." Zeke squinted up at Jed with a sly smile, winking one dark eye. "I could always go for some wet heat."

"Simmer down." Jed chuckled.

"I'm just sayin', we haven't had the pleasure of a sporting house in quite a spell."

"I know it, too." Jed stirred the pot of beans on the fire as the memory of desire stirred elsewhere. "It's been exactly twenty-three days, but who's counting?"

"Twenty-three?" Zeke whistled between his teeth. "No wonder I'm so ornery as of late."

"As of late?"

"Quiet," Zeke muttered, placing his hat over his wide, friendly face to block out the sun.

Travis and Tom sat around the fire, the horses fed and watered. "Feels like a storm in the air," Tom observed, tipping back his hat to mop sweat from his brow.

The others agreed and fell into conversation led by Zeke about what they'd get into the next time they hit town. There was little question as to what he wanted to get up to, and it took roughly no time at all for the boys to agree with him.

Jed kept to himself, as he tended to do in these situations.

Not that he was against a man having his share of fun at the sporting house—he'd been through enough of them himself, and no woman had ever been the worse for having known him. But he wouldn't make up the sort of stories his three traveling partners liked to share, about the ladies who worked inside being so overwhelmed by their prowess that they'd refused payment.

No whore refused payment. That simply wasn't how things were done. And they certainly didn't call their friends into the room afterward, that they might get a turn.

But he was content with smiling and nodding, pretending to go along with the tall tales his friends spun.

His mind was elsewhere, anyway. He got that way whenever they took too long between jobs. It had been two weeks at Jake's count since their last job, which had provided them with enough gold to suit them for quite a spell.

But it wasn't enough. It was never enough to quit.

And when he had too much time on his hands, he had time to think.

Thinking was not a good thing for a man like him. It led him down dark paths he would rather avoid altogether if possible.

Sometimes he remembered the ranch and wondered what would've happened if the war never came and there was a way for him to get home before the land got parceled out and sold off. He had never been back.

When the sun sank in a ball of crimson and disappeared behind the distant mountains, it reminded him so much of those days—those sunsets, long ago and long forgotten by everyone but him—that he sometimes felt a pain in his chest.

As he did at that moment.

Where would he be just then, right that very minute, if that terrible day had never come and life had continued in the same direction it had started? He'd have gone to war, certainly, but then?

He might be enjoying supper with his family, with the sunset a ball of fire outside the dining room window. A charming wife, a saucy daughter, a son who'd ask too many questions and want to be part of everything he thought would make him a man.

Just like Jasper had been.

Jed Cunningham knew he was in a bad way when he started thinking about Jasper.

They settled in to eat, and Jed was grateful for the break in the chatter. When the three of them got going, they were worse than a circle of old biddies in their rockers, cackling over their knitting needles.

Only old biddies never talked about the sorts of things Zeke, Tom, and Travis did.

At least, Jed imagined so. He grinned to himself at the idea that perhaps they did. After all, old biddies weren't born old, were they? There had to be at least one or two good stories among a group of them.

He soaked up the juice from the beans with a piece of dried biscuit. They were sorely low on supplies, and that was a fact, down to the last few cans of beans and a little flour and salt. He did what he could when it was his turn to cook, but he was no miracle worker.

"I imagine we'll have to head to town soon," he observed, watching Zeke from the corner of his eye. "But no funny stuff."

His friend's face fell. "Why not?" he asked, reminding Jed of how his brother used to sound when he found out he couldn't have his way—back when his brother was maybe five or six years of age, not twenty years older.

Jasper would never be Zeke's age or anything older than ten. He'd been ten for a dozen years or more.

Travis spoke up, so Jed didn't have to. "You know the rules, same as the rest of us. We don't show our faces around so close to a job, so no one there will remember us passing through."

"Right," Tom added. "Going to the mercantile for food supplies or a new pair of boot is one thing, but whoopin' it up with a house full of gals the way you like to do, well..."

"I could behave myself," Zeke argued, which earned him a round of hearty laughter.

"Might be you could," Jed nodded once he could speak again, "but you won't. Not once those beauties come at you with their smiles and their sweet talk."

"It ain't the smiles nor the sweet talk that interests me," he grumbled, folding his thick arms over an equally thick stomach.

"No, and it ain't your charm or your skill in bed that gets them interested in you," Travis replied with a wry grin, which got them laughing again.

"Oh, because they're fallin' all over themselves to rub up on you," Zeke snorted.

Travis cocked an eyebrow.

Everyone knew how sensitive he was about only one thing—Jed supposed he'd been a looker in his younger days, before pieces of a wagon full of dynamite had torn into his face back in '63. He liked to keep his hat low when they rode and rarely allowed himself to be seen near areas where they'd be pulling a job. He was too easy to identify.

"It ain't my face they're interested in, and I know it," he murmured. "But once I drop my drawers, they find out I didn't hurt nothin' below the waist."

"I thought you said they find out you didn't have nothin' below the waist," Tom laughed.

Travis punched his shoulder.

Jed chuckled along with the rest of them, including Travis—he could laugh at himself, something the rest of them had difficulty with.

Even so, his heart wasn't in his laughter. It was someplace else. He was getting fidgety, wanting to move on. He got this way whenever he started feeling low about things. Impatient, unsatisfied.

They went silent when the cry of a coyote sounded in the distance, then another. The horses went still, their ears trained in the direction of the call.

"S'all right," Jed said, going to them. "Ain't no coyote comin' near our camp."

He'd always felt a coyote's call was a rather mournful sound. There were times when it made him feel awful lonesome. Like just then, even surrounded by friends and partners. He could still feel alone when surrounded by people.

Not that he could ever tell them about it. They'd look at him like he'd smoked some of that funny plant that made men go off their rockers.

Maybe he had gone off his rocker some. Maybe that was his problem in a nutshell. He was twenty-eight years old, and he had nothing to show for all those years. Other men had businesses of their own, farms or ranches, wives, and babies. Something real.

He didn't even have a home. Home was the outdoors, or the tent if he was feeling poorly or the weather was too rough. Sometimes they would stay atop a saloon if they weren't pulling a job too close to town, just passing through. If they had the money for it.

There were times when he felt his mother's eyes peering down at him from Heaven, and when he had that feeling he'd want to die of shame over what she had to be thinking of him.

The firelight dimmed behind him, telling him Zeke was putting it out. It was time to pack up and get ready for work.

They fell into their normal routine without saying much. They didn't have to speak, each of them having gone through it enough times that they might have been able to do it in their sleep.

Travis stripped the horses of everything but their bridles and saddles, loading all of the packs into the wagon which they'd already half-hidden in a cluster of tall rocks while Zeke and Tom cleared the supper mess and Jed made sure there was nothing left behind to prove they'd been camping there.

By the time they mounted up and walked the horses for a bit to warm them up, the light had gone completely out of the sky, and a big, bright moon lit the dry plains of North Texas. There was nothing but hard-packed clay, spotty bits of grass and brush as far as the eye could see until one reached the hills to the west, where elms and oaks grew thick.

They started off north, riding at an easy pace but hardly dawdling. Those Butterfield coaches rode all through the day and almost all the night, and they were known to move faster than any other stagecoach line in the west, perhaps in the country.

And they were looking to stop one, which meant they had to be ready and waiting for it to approach.

They waited two-by-two on opposite sides of the dusty road, waiting for the first sign of it in the distance. The moonlight worked in their favor, though it would mean making themselves visible to the driver and the man riding shotgun.

All of them reached for the kerchiefs, tied them, so nothing but their eyes were visible—and even then, Jed liked to go about business with his head low, the brim of his black hat covering the rest of his face in case anybody got too curious about his looks.

Though the presence of a pistol generally wiped out all such curiosity. He'd found that through many such hold-ups all along the Butterfield route, the Wells Fargo and others. Anything they could stop, they did stop, and they took the occupants for everything they had.

It was almost too easy sometimes, and too easy to ride off while those he'd stolen from wondered what to do next.

It was easy to forget they were people like him. Except for the money. They could do without their money, their watches and rings and purses. He, on the other hand, needed the money to live.

Though the question of what type of life he was living never strayed far from his mind, try though he might to get it out of there.

A low whistle from the other side of the road told him

Tom had spotted something in the distance. Jed checked his pistol once more to ensure it was ready to go, then began walking the horse at a brisk trot to warm it before coaxing it into a run as the coach drew closer.

This was it. Time to earn his living.

3

"**A**re you feeling quite well?"

Melissa opened her eyes, groggy, searching for the source of the voice which had woken her. The inside of the coach was black as pitch, telling her at least the general time of day, if not the particular hour.

It was the kindly man to her right whose name she still did not know. He kept to himself during their brief rest stops, just as she had, his head down while the rest of the men spoke of things which Melissa had little care for and therefore paid little attention to.

Mealtime was time to eat, and memories of gnawing, ever-present hunger were like a ghost which shadowed her no matter where she went. Each meal placed a bit more space between the ghost and herself, so she busied her mouth with the act of chewing and swallowing.

She wondered if this man was the same, or if he merely

wished to keep to himself. There were times when she wished all of her traveling companions were the same. What she would not have given for pure, unbroken silence.

She blinked hard, striving to clear the heaviness in her head and answer the man who sounded so concerned. "I believe so. Did I give you reason to believe otherwise?"

He chuckled. "Why, yes, ma'am. You were groanin' like."

Groaning. Why had she groaned?

Oh. Yes.

The dream came rushing back. So similar to so many others.

"I did not know I made noise in my sleep. I am quite embarrassed," she admitted. "And I do humbly apologize if I disturbed you."

He merely smiled, the thin beams of moonlight which shone in through the square window revealing his shining teeth. "A man can't get a decent stretch of sleep while being tossed back and forth, now can he?"

She looked around the coach, where it appeared the other passengers were sleeping, chins touching chests.

Her companion chuckled. "All right, then. I can't sleep while gettin' tossed around."

She smiled. He was a nice man, and she'd known so few of them. It got to the point where she'd doubted their existence.

"Just the same," she murmured, "I am sorry for being a bother."

"Bad dreams?" He fixed a shrewd eye upon her.

She nodded. No sense in lying to the man who'd heard her in the throes of brutal memory. "Sometimes, yes."

"Wouldn't wonder. Most folks have nightmares since the war. You're from up north, aren't you?"

She nodded.

"I suppose your memories of the war are a bit different from those in the Confederacy," he mused, nodding slowly. "But war is war and privation is privation no matter which side of the fightin' you happen to be on."

"I suppose." Though her privation had little to do with the war between the states. As far as she'd been concerned, there might as well have been no war, for it had not made much difference to her family. Her father long dead, her brothers too young to fight.

No, life had been much the same horror during those bloody years as it had been before.

"What takes you out west, then?" he asked. "Your husband waitin' for you?"

"Yes." She turned the familiar gold band around and around, accustomed to its pressure. "On our ranch. I was back east to visit family."

"I see. He must be anxiously awaitin' a pretty thing like yourself."

For perhaps the first time in her life, Melissa felt flattered at a man's compliment. For once, she did not consider her sky-blue eyes or creamy skin a liability. He did not cause her skin to crawl as so many had over the years, ever since she had developed into a woman.

And even before then.

For, while a beautiful lady was a joy to all those who gazed upon her, she was a joy to be treasured from afar. Something untouchable.

While a poor girl whose clothes were little more than rags and whose mother was known to entertain men for money was something for everyone to enjoy—or so they'd clearly believed. She'd been something to look at with a lustful eye, to sneer at and treat as though she ought to be grateful for any little bit of attention.

"I believe my husband has been far too concerned with the affairs of the ranch to worry himself with thoughts of me," she demurred.

"Then you don't know much about men, pardon my sayin'."

"Perhaps I don't."

They shared a secret smile, the sort shared by two people who hadn't much experience sharing their thoughts with another and who delighted in the presence of another gentle soul.

"You go to sleep now, ma'am," he said. "You look as though you need it. Won't no harm come to you here, with all these men about you and that burly mountain of a fella ridin' shotgun. Just rest your head."

She thanked him with a smile and allowed her head to rest against the coach wall once again. Sleep would not come, and she knew it. Not for quite a while, at least. When the sky began to lighten, and the memories faded back as they always did in the morning, sleep might overtake her again.

It had been two weeks since she'd left Boston on just such a night, warm and clear, with nothing but the clothes she'd brought with her on the day of her wedding, and the letters and tickets for the stagecoach.

She had no wish for John Carter to accuse her of taking anything from him. Nothing he had purchased for her during their year-long marriage made it to the trip. It all sat in the hope chest he'd presented to her after the wedding.

Hope chest. What a strange name. She might have held hope in those early days. Hope she would no longer starve. Hope she would manage a decent household, not the sort she'd grown up in—scrimping for every last bit of food or money, struggling to keep her three brothers from getting themselves killed while they stole and begged on the streets.

Hope for peace at last. A warm bed, a full night's sleep, to wake up without dread in her heart over what the day may bring.

Those hopes lasted all of three days.

Until John Carter showed her the type of man he truly was. When his kind, dark eyes had gone hard, never to soften again.

She squeezed her eyes shut, willing away the memory of the blows, the shouts, the accusations of laziness and infidelity while she knew very well where he spent his evenings. The fact that he'd managed the stamina to get her with child was almost impressive.

Her hands crossed over her belly. Oh, the baby. How she had warred with herself over the happiness and horror.

For she'd always wanted a baby of her own. Someone to love her, someone to belong to her. Nobody had ever done either—her mama might have in the early days, when life was easier, and she had a husband to rely on, but it was difficult to love somebody who meant nothing more than another mouth to feed.

Love was a luxury. There had been no luxury in their lives.

And so, when she'd understood the truth of her situation, the day she'd recognized her missed courses and the fatigue which suddenly plagued her, the aversion to coffee and foods which she had once enjoyed, she'd first experienced a flash of wonder.

She'd never had a wish come true before.

In that instant, she'd imagined everything her child might become.

Before John Carter's face had filled her mind and put all of her dreams to rest.

A cold chill had filled her then, leaving her shaking, holding onto the bedpost for support. What if he killed the child before it was born? What if the child's crying infuriated him and he beat it as he so regularly beat her? His cruelty would surely not stop at his wife, for he was a cruel man by nature.

One single, clear thought had occurred to her then.

She would have to marry the man with whom she'd

corresponded, rather than simply using the ticket he sent her to get away from Boston.

Even with a husband who was only a husband in name, one who beat and belittled and treated her as little more than a slave without allowing her so much as a cent to her name, Melissa battled bitter guilt at her deception.

She remembered finding the ad in the newspaper, one for a bride willing to set up house with a rancher in Nevada. It had been the morning after a particularly difficult night, John had come home from the sporting house in a fouler temper than usual.

How her mind had whirled at the possibilities the ad presented. A new life, all the way on the other side of the country. Somewhere John could never find her.

No one need know of her past. Her shame, the sort of shame that could not be erased by a gold wedding band and a man's name attached to her own. Shame such as hers could not be washed away with the strongest soap.

She would change her name, find a job—Carson City was a booming town, full of possibility, there were bound to be positions available in the mercantile or the post office or some such place. She could support herself for the first time, just herself, without younger half-siblings hanging on, without a mother now too sickly much of the time to do more than lie in bed.

Freedom.

She could taste it before she'd even laid pen to paper.

His first letter had been a source of greater guilt, for

Mark Furnish seemed like a good man. Hard-working, determined, full of vitality and big dreams. He might easily have painted a rosy image of ranch life in hopes of luring her, but he had not.

He had not been aware of her desperation, either, or how promptly she would accept.

The morning she'd found out about the child, she had already sent a letter in reply, telling him she would be pleased to move to Carson City and become his bride. She'd waited with bated breath every time the post arrived, waiting for the envelope containing the tickets for the train to St. Louis and the stagecoach which would carry her the remainder of the way.

She had even requested he purchase them in the name of Mrs. Mark Furnish—for she could not travel under her married name, as John might be clever enough to find her if she did. She'd reasoned with her would-be husband that a married woman would be less likely to suffer the attentions of men along the journey than an unmarried girl.

And she had hoped he'd believed her.

By the time the tickets had arrived—under the name she'd requested—she'd known about the child for four days. Four days she'd spent avoiding her husband at all costs, so as to lessen the chance of him beating her.

The following night, she'd made her escape while he was asleep, intoxicated enough to never notice the opening of the downstairs door.

She had never intended to marry Mark until the presence of the baby had become clear. That one tiny wrinkle in her plans had changed everything. For the shame she'd borne as a poor girl with a soiled dove for a mother had been nothing compared to what her bastard brothers had endured and likely still endured after her marriage. Poor pups, without a father's name behind their own.

Even if they labored to pull themselves from poverty, what could they ever become? Society spat upon the father-less, as though the circumstances behind a child's existence were any fault of theirs.

Melissa vowed then and there, that first morning, that she would never allow her child to be called a bastard.

It meant marrying Mark, then. There was no other way. She could never allow John Carter to stake a claim on the child, for she could never escape him if that were the case. He would not let a child of his get away from him, and she would have eaten broken glass before she'd leave her child alone with him for a father. She would—

"Hey, there! You! What do you think you're doin'?"

For an instant, Melissa thought it was John who shouted. John who fired a rifle. She jumped at the second cracking sound, covering her ears, realizing in an instant that she'd been asleep again and that it was not her husband who was shouting, who'd fired a gun.

It was the men riding up front, driving the team.

"What's happening?" she screamed as they sped up, the coach bouncing so she thought it might fall apart. Her hands flailed about for something to hold onto, and the man beside her allowed her to clutch his arm.

He spoke only one word which rose above the din both in the coach and inside Melissa's head. "Robbers."

No. Her baby. What if they harmed the baby?

The horses ran as though the devil himself were after them, and he might very well have been. There were noises other than the horrible squealing of the wheels and axles as they flew over the prairie.

Whoops. Shouts. Gunfire.

Suddenly, the coach jerked violently to the left, sending the passengers—including Melissa, who sat on the left—flying in that direction. It was a blessing her new friend withstood most of the weight of the man to his right, for the two of them could have crushed her otherwise.

This was it. She was going to die in the middle of Texas without ever reaching the chance to start a new life. All of the suffering she'd endured, all of the dreams she'd dared to dream once the notion of escape became a reality, all of it would come to nothing.

Only then did the coach begin to slow, until it came to a hard stop, pitching its occupants forward this time.

"This coach and everything it carries belongs to us now." A strident male voice, rang out above the confusion and groans of discomfort as the men sorted themselves out.

Melissa wondered if she was the only one who heard that voice over the others. Who heard and understood what it meant.

The door flung open then, revealing a tall man wearing a black hat and a kerchief around the lower half of his face.

She could see nothing of him thanks to the shadow the hat's brim cast over his eyes.

"Out of the coach," he ordered, his voice harsh.

He gestured with one hand, causing moonlight to glint off the metal of his pistol.

Dread coiled and uncoiled in her stomach. The half-spoiled potatoes they'd eaten for supper hours earlier threatened to come up as the men exited the coach one by one. They left her for last, as she sat in the far corner.

The sight of the pistol had all but frozen her solid, even as good sense urged her to move. What if the outlaw holding it became impatient with her slowness?

As if he heard her, the man peered into the coach. "Hurry it up, now! We haven't got all night!"

A second voice, somewhat familiar. "You might at least help the lady from the coach." After that, a sound like an armful of clothing hitting the floor and a strangled groan.

Mr. Lang. They'd struck him for speaking out. The animals.

This, more than anything else that had happened so far, inspired Melissa to slide her way over the bench and the bags of mail bulging out from beneath. She did so quickly, now determined to give someone a piece of her mind.

To strike a man whose only desire was to speak up for her? Someone who'd behaved like a gentleman?

When she reached the door, her narrowed eyes took in the scene—her eight fellow travelers, all of them with hands in the air except for Mr. Lang. He had fallen to one knee, arms crossed over his stomach.

What concerned her more was the second man on his knees, some distance behind the coach. Where they had taken the sharp turn which had nearly resulted in her being crushed. She recognized him as the man who'd been riding next to the driver. And now, he knelt next to the driver.

Who was on his back in a spreading pool of blood.

"Come on, come on." A strong hand seized her arm, pulled her along until she stood at the end of the row of men, beside Mr. Lang.

Two men looted the coach, taking what appeared valuable and stashing it in leather satchels. A third man stood guard nearby, rifle at the ready.

The one who'd opened the door and ordered them out looked up and down the line, his eyes still concealed by his hat brim. "Gimme your valuables. Now. Be quick about it."

For once, Melissa was relieved to possess nothing of any value. If they wanted her wedding band, they could have it —she'd only worn it to further the deceit of her being Mrs. Mark Furnish. She would otherwise have left it on her bedside table.

Poor Mr. Lang looked ready to weep as he handed over his pocket watch. Melissa bit her tongue against the sharp words the robbers deserved to hear.

"What about you?" The robber stood in front of the kind old man who'd likely saved her life—or at least the life of her child, protecting her from injury in the coach.

"I ain't got nothin' you're wantin'," he announced. "Some chewin' tobacco, that's about it."

The man guarding the coach snorted. "He's lying."

"I ain't a liar," the old man snarled, glaring at the rifle-toting brute who stormed his way, delivering a hearty blow to his midsection with the butt of the gun.

As far as Melissa was concerned, this was the breaking point. With a cry of outrage, she marched over to the men. "How dare you?" she shrieked.

Only then did her eyes meet those of the pistol-wielding robber. Flinty gray, sharp and searing. "You had better step aside," he muttered.

She whirled on the man with the rifle. "It takes no courage for a bigger, stronger, younger man with a rifle to harm an innocent old gentleman like this! You ought to be ashamed of yourselves!"

Only then did the possibility of earning such rough treatment occur. A rifle butt to the stomach might kill her baby, stays or no stays.

Still, she held her head high, staring at the brute as if daring him to defy her. For one breathless moment, she hung between certainty that he would strike her and certainty of his not having the gall to do any such thing.

To her relief, it was the latter.

"This one has spirit!" the man laughed, nasty and knowing. She'd heard that sort of laughter before, and it meant little to her.

"Mrs. Furnish, do not trouble yourself," the old man urged, touching her shoulder while still half-bent, the other arm across his middle. "It ain't worth it."

The flinty-eyed robber startled. "Mrs. Furnish, you say?"

"Yes," she lied in her most imperious tone.

"As in, the wife of Mr. Mark Furnish? The rancher?"

"You've heard of him?"

"Ain't a man west of the Mississippi who ain't, ma'am." He turned to his partner. "I think this just turned out to be a very profitable night."

4

She was a pretty little thing, this rancher's wife. Dressed plain, but Jed guessed that had to do more with keeping her from getting noticed by men such as himself.

A well-dressed woman traveling in a stagecoach was bound to attract the wrong kind of attention, and Mark Furnish was a smart man. A man didn't get where he ended up without being smart about such things.

Even in that ratty bonnet, there was no hiding her golden hair. Or the flashing blue eyes, the way anger brought roses to her cheeks.

He turned to Zeke once again, wondering if his friend understood what he was getting at. It was not a surprise to find confusion in the brown eyes barely visible over the top of his kerchief.

With his pistol aimed in the general direction of the woman before him—he had no desire to shoot the woman, especially when she could mean a handsome payday, he motioned for Zeke to lean in.

"He's rich, her husband," he muttered, always watching the woman and the men around her. Cowards, the lot of them, as most men were. All they need do to tamp down any foolish ideas about bravery was to glance in the direction of the dying driver, out there on the road.

It was not Jed's wish to kill the man, and had the fool not attempted to bring the team about and run him clean over, he would not have fired. It was more a panic shot than anything else, though he would've rather bit off his tongue than admit it to any of the others.

Regrettable as it was, the fool's death served as a reminder to the rest that they'd best stay put and mind their manners, or else the same treatment might be theirs.

"Yeah?" Zeke asked, suddenly interested.

"You never heard of him?"

"Eh, I thought I heard the name before, but you know I don't keep up with such matters." This was true, and something Jed should have known. Unless speaking of the weather and how it would affect their work, the nearest saloon or sporting house, or the next time they planned to eat, Zeke cared little.

"Well, I can tell you, the man runs one of the biggest outfits in Nevada. He might be one of the richest men in the whole state. And she's his wife."

"Oh, really now?" The sly excitement in his friend's voice told Jed a flame had begun to flicker, at last. While it took Zeke a moment to pick up, once he did, Jed knew he was reliable.

He went to Tom and Travis to share the idea of taking the woman, while Jed focused his gaze on the feisty little thing. She possessed courage, he had to admit. Coming to an old man's defense while another man lay dying as the result of a slug to the gut.

She had no way of knowing how the exchange would turn out, yet she'd reacted.

"You headed home, then, ma'am?" he asked, tilting his head back a bit that he might see her without the brim of his hat in the way. Yes, she was right pretty. And right furious.

"What of it?" she demanded. "I might be much closer to home now, if it weren't for you. We were no bother to anyone, simply looking to get where we were heading."

She didn't speak as though she was from the south or the plains. A northerner. Her accent was sort of flat, like those northerners spoke. So Furnish had married a Yankee gal. Probably wanted somebody with an education and manners and the like.

Though the woman in front of him did not seem to care much for manners. She was fixing to work herself into a downright frenzy.

"You're all a bunch of heartless, cowardly brutes! Shooting an unarmed man simply trying to do his job. Striking unarmed men to get them to fall in line with you." She sneered, one of her full, rose petal lips curling up. "You're all despicable."

"Quite a mouth on you, seein' as how I'm holding a pistol, ma'am." He merely tipped his hat to her, a gesture which only seemed to wind her up more. She was quite a bit of fun.

It got tiresome, speaking and riding and camping out with the same three men day after day. There were entire weeks when he saw nothing but flat, dry desert with little in the way of entertainment. She was a breath of fresh air after just such a spell.

One of the men in line cleared his throat. The one who just lost his pocket watch—a beautiful thing, truly, something Jed would very much enjoy carrying.

"What do you intend to do now?" he asked in a trembling voice, though it was clear he tried very hard for it not to be so.

"None of your business, and if you don't stop speakin' when you haven't been spoken to, you'll find yourself with broken ribs this time." Jed made it a point to look the woman in the eye after he said it, smiling under his kerchief at the way her cheeks went dark again.

He could just imagine the sort of passion a woman like her possessed. What she might be stirred to, given the right attention.

She did not let go of his gaze, in fact, judging by the way her jaw hardened and her eyes narrowed, he felt she might know exactly what was on his mind. How could she? Perhaps he was feeling a bit guilty for harboring such thought about another man's wife.

Though it would be the first time for any such jolt of

conscience, but he'd always heard there was a first time for everything.

Zeke returned. "They're in," he muttered. "And they took everything they could find from the coach. Not much, but there are some fine cigars."

Jed shrugged. "We got more than enough from the passengers." They'd collected each man's billfold, and some of them had been full to the point of bulging. When would people figure out the need to travel light? For surely Jed and his crew were not the only ones riding the plains, waiting to catch stagecoach drivers unaware.

"Come on, then." He reached for the woman's arm, which she was quick to yank away.

A cry rose out from among the men.

"Now, just wait a minute!" one of them called out, charging forward.

Zeke need only step in front of the man, rifle aimed at his gut, to get him to stand down.

"You might have us outnumbered, but we have you outgunned," Jed reminded them, this time taking the woman by the waist. She squirmed, her body rubbing against his, and he did mightily wish she would cease.

It was one thing to command a group of men to do as he wished, and another to do so while stirring between his thighs.

"How dare you!" She all but clawed at his eyes in the struggle to free herself, but Jed was stronger. He held her fast while wrapping her wrists in a length of rope he always hung from his belt before mounting, then hauling her up into his lap.

And still, she screamed, elbowed, kicked out with her rather worn leather shoes. This was the only thing Jed took umbrage with. "I don't mind you kickin' me," he grunted, "but do not kick my horse. He did nothing to you."

To his surprise, her legs stopped moving. He thought she might possess a bit of sense, after all.

"Meet you at the wagon," he called to Zeke before taking off in a cloud of dust. Best to get her out of there as soon as possible, in case any of the others started feeling brave.

Her shouts faded to nothing more than muffled protests once the pounding of hooves drowned them out. A blessing.

For now, he needed to figure out what to do with her, and in order to do that, he needed to be able to think.

5

I t was the last thing she'd expected.

At the very worst, she had imagined giving up her wedding band. She'd have done so gladly, seeing as how the gold circle had never brought her anything but grief since the day John had jammed it onto her finger in a pitifully quick ceremony held in his parlor.

They had not even gone to the Justice of the Peace, much less rung the chapel bell.

It would have been no great hardship to be without that one last memory of her ill-fated marriage—well, not counting the fluttering bit of life inside her.

But this? This, being pawed at and manhandled? Tied up? Swept away into the night on the back of a horse her captor had more than likely stolen?

This was the stuff of nightmares—only she'd never possessed the imagination to dream up anything so very dangerous.

Where was he taking her? She could hardly see for the dust and finally had no choice but to turn her head to the side, allowing her bonnet to cover her face. This left her with no view whatsoever, though she knew it mattered little whether or not she could see.

It wasn't as though she knew where they were or where they were going.

And she certainly had no control over their direction, hands bound as tight as they were. She could hardly feel her fingers, much less take control of the beast on which she rode if her captor fell from the saddle.

How she would laugh if that happened. Then again, he held the end of the rope which bound her wrists, meaning he would pull her along with him.

There was simply no way out of her horrible predicament. Once again, life had happened to her, and she had no choice but to suffer its whims.

They came to a rather abrupt stop quite a way from the scene of the robbery, having ridden for endless minutes at a pace which had all but shaken her senseless. A series of boulders sat in a semi-circle.

"What are we doing now?" she asked, a tremor creeping into her voice as she imagined a number of things men might do to women in secluded areas such as this, with nothing but the moon and an out-of-breath horse to bear witness.

He did not answer. He merely took her by the waist upon dismounting and pulled her to the ground. When she threw her body against his and tried to run, he merely stood still, feet rooted to the spot.

As though he were one of the boulders he stood before.

He might as well have been, for all she was concerned. He had no feeling, no kindness. He would allow his men—for he was the leader, it was plain as day—to harm a defenseless old man. He would encourage them to steal from strangers.

He would kill a man in cold blood.

She raised her bound wrists and brought them down upon his shoulder as he dragged her behind the boulders.

"I hate you!" she snarled, hitting him again and again. "You are a lowly, cowardly, pitiful creature unworthy of the air you breathe!"

To her surprise, he chuckled, which only served to further infuriate her. She could hardly breathe for the rage boiling in her veins.

She'd never experience this before. This head-spinning, heart-pounding sensation. Anger, yes. She'd felt anger—deep, hot, seething anger. Fear, of course. Resentment, bitterness, resignation.

Envy.

All of it, for about as long as she could recall.

But this? This rage? She had never even been stirred to such depths during her marriage, and heaven knew her husband had deserved it.

Only when she saw what was behind the boulders did she remember to breathe. A wagon. They'd hidden it there, out of sight, somewhat safe, unhitched.

"Get up there." He took her by the waist without so much as a warning and lifted her into the rear of the wagon, dropping her with a thud so hard it knocked the bonnet from her head.

"That hurt!" she snapped, though he'd dropped her on her backside and she could think of worse ways to land. Even so, he needed to know the depth of her outrage.

"You're lucky I didn't throw you in," he muttered as he led the horse to the front of the wagon. He'd untied the kerchief and exposed the rest of his face, though she could make little of it in the shadow of the boulders.

"So you do speak? I thought you'd forgotten how."

"Yeah. I speak."

She could see nothing of his face while he tilted his head down as he did just then.

"Why are you doing this? What reason is there to take me as you have?" Desperation crept into her voice, and she did not like the sound of it, not one bit, but this was a desperate situation. Exceptions could be made.

He glanced up, but she could still see nothing of his eyes. "What do you think the reason is? You talk like a smart Yankee gal. You tell me."

She blushed. No one had ever called her smart. "You want to take me along with you and... keep me for your group."

His laughter echoed off the boulders, carrying away into the night sky. "Lord, you Yankees have some high-toned ideas, don't you?"

"What does that mean?" she demanded.

"Do you think I need to kidnap women and ravish them against their will? Is that what you think?"

In spite of his chuckling and the burning, tingling sensation all through her face and neck, she scoffed. "No. I would never think such a thing of a man who was able to kill another man as you did. Why would I make such a guess? How silly of me."

Though she still could not see his eyes, she could feel them as he glared at her. A sliver of moonlight touched the side of his face, revealing a lean cheek covered in dark stubble and a sharp jaw.

"Enough talk, Yankee gal."

"I have a name."

He finished hitching the horse and swept a low, formal bow. "Forgive me. Mrs. Furnish."

She merely turned her face away, as this was not her name and the using of it made her uncomfortable. "You know him? Mr. Furnish?"

"I know of him, like I said. And I wonder why he would let his wife travel all alone, but that's not for me to say." He snorted. "And I thought I said no more talking."

That was all right with her, for she had more than enough to think over.

There were four of them—and from what she'd seen, the leader was the smart one. The other three seemed more the muscle, the ones who threatened violence while the man waiting for their return was the thinker, the planner.

He would be a challenge to slip past, if she could slip

past him at all. Every man had to sleep at some time, did he not? She would have to rely on that, then.

He thought she was the lady of Furnish Ranch. Would this influence his treatment? Would he be kinder, gentler, more tolerant? It was clear from his tone of voice that he cared little for her intended—was that personal, or simply an attitude he held regarding all wealthy men?

She would wager on the latter. He was a thief, after all, and a violent one. He would think little of wealthy, self-made men who had achieved such success that his name was recognizable as far out as north Texas.

If that was where they were.

"Where are we?" She shifted on her backside, her arms useless—they were beginning to numb as her hands already had, but she managed to work her way across the wooden boards of the wagon to where the robber waited on the bench, holding onto the horse's reins.

"What does it matter?" His gaze remained fixed on the horizon. He was waiting for his partners.

"Because I have to get to Carson City. It's of the greatest urgency." Every day that passed meant another day closer to delivery and less chance of Mark believing her child to be his own.

"We'll get there."

"When?"

"When we get there."

"That isn't good enough!"

"It'll have to be!" He threw a look over his shoulder, hard and cold and uncaring, his face still half-hidden beneath the brim of his hat. She imagined his mouth would be thin, lips drawn together in a thin line as he scowled.

"My husband is waiting for me. He will send the law looking for me."

"He'll get you back when we're good and ready to deliver you. And by then, he'll be ready to pay what we say he'll pay."

Her breath released in a long, gusty sigh. So that was it. They would ransom her. They believed she was his wife— as she'd wanted them to—and assumed this meant he would pay a great deal of money to reclaim her.

What would they think if they knew she was not married—at least, not to the rancher?

Would they even care?

Likely not, as a man might still be willing to pay for his fiancée. They'd already gone through the trouble of kidnapping her, and they might as well go through with the plan.

At least, that is how she would have proceeded if she were in their place.

Which she would never be, as they were beyond reproach. While she had grown up poor, all but spat on by "proper" society, she would never have stooped to the depths this man stooped to. Not even if it meant warding off starvation.

The question then became whether Mark Furnish would be willing to pay for her. He was a good man, she'd known it from his letter. But how easy would it be for a man to merely feign kindness? Who in his right mind would convey cruelty in a letter to a prospective wife?

Melissa knew all too well how quickly a man could change. As though he'd only been wearing a mask of civility, concealing the monster beneath. Lulling the woman he'd married into a false sense of security, like a snake just waiting to strike.

And strike he had.

The robber raised his head when two figures appeared on the horizon. Only two, silhouetted by moonlight as they raced across the flat, open land.

Melissa watched them while glancing his way from time to time. This did not bode well for him.

"What are they doin'?" he muttered.

"Do you think it's the law?" she asked, hoping against hope.

"Be quiet," he snarled. "Don't forget I have a six shooter here. I can shut you up pretty quick."

She held her tongue. If it had been just her, she would not have practiced such caution. What did it matter if he killed her? She'd never cared much for her own life. In fact, he would be doing her a favor.

Only it was not a matter of her alone, and she needed to keep this in mind.

"What happened?" The robber stood, reins in hand, while his partners came to a stop in a cloud of dust.

The very large one, the one who'd held the rifle on the men, shook his head as he dismounted. "A ruckus. One of 'em took it in his head to put up a fight, punched Tom. Two of 'em jumped him, and they tussled, managed to get the gun from him."

Melissa did not know whether to cheer or weep, for she knew this could not have ended well.

"What then?"

"Shot 'im," the other replied as he dismounted, clutching his arm. "He's gone."

The leader sat with a thud that shook the wagon.

"Don't worry," the wounded man replied. "We paid 'em back."

Melissa bit her tongue against the impulse to demand to know what they'd done. Besides, she knew, didn't she? Two of the men from the coach were dead, along with the driver.

Why had they fought? They might have gone on, reported the robbery at the next stage. Why were men so stupid? Was it their pride? Could they not live with themselves knowing they'd allowed a group of armed bandits to get the better of them?

They would not have to live with themselves now.

She sank into the wagon, lying on her side with her knees drawn up and tears in her eyes, mourning men she'd never known while cursing their foolishness.

And reminding herself all the while of the viciousness around her. This could serve as a lesson, she realized. These were not men to be trifled with.

Once a second horse was hitched, the large man with the rifle joined the leader at the front of the wagon while the third man rode horseback in spite of his injured arm.

Melissa peered at him over the side of the wagon, noting the way he favored his shoulder. This did not stop him from moving on any more than the loss of one of their partners did.

They simply kept moving, along with their helpless captive.

6

J ed could hardly see straight for the rage buzzing around in his head.

He ought to have known better than to leave the three of them alone. Why had he done it? What possessed him? All they needed to do was mount up and ride away.

Now, Tom was dead. The stupid, hotheaded fool. Jed had always known he'd get himself killed, but like this? In such a useless manner? Overtaken by a pair of men he'd already picked clean?

He peered at Zeke, sitting to his right with the rifle across his legs. What had they not told him? For truly, it was their word alone, which he had to go on.

There had to be more to the story. One of them started a fight or hit one of their victims just for the hell of it. Something. They tended to get out of hand when there was no one near to keep them in line.

He'd allowed men to die—including one of his own. He ought to have been there with them to prevent such a thing from happening, but he'd run off with the Yankee, instead.

He was just as much a fool as any of them.

"You all right?" Zeke asked as the wagon bumped and bounced, their horses working as a team to carry them onward.

"No. I am truly not." He glanced over his shoulder to be sure the woman wasn't listening in. "That went to hell, and you know it."

"This is the way it goes sometimes."

"Not for us," Jed snarled. "Never for us. You all shoulda been outta there no more than a minute after I was. Why did you linger?"

"So it's our fault? Is that what you mean to say?"

Jed counted to five, forced himself to take a deep breath. While he and Zeke had always seen eye-to-eye, nothing such as this had ever tested their bond before. Though his partner was a jovial fellow, always looking to have a good time, he also bore a nasty streak as wide as the plains.

It would do no good to have him as an enemy.

He took another tack. "I only wish I understood what went wrong this time that never went wrong before."

Zeke's face brightened some, like clouds had parted to let the sun shine through. "Aw, shoot. That's easy. We never had anybody fight back before."

Jed mulled this over and saw the truth of it. Whereas they'd been called just about every dirty name in the book and more than a few he'd never heard before, even though they'd been spat at and on and shot nasty looks that could freeze boiling water, nobody had ever fought back.

Hell, he'd seen men make water in their trousers, but he'd never met a man or woman who didn't clam up real fast at the sight of a pistol.

Suddenly, he understood, and the knowing of it all but made him slam on the brake and kick the Yankee gal clear out of the wagon. "It was her."

"Huh?"

"The woman. We never took a woman before, either, did we? That was why they fought. For her."

Zeke scratched his stubble-covered chin, then chuckled. "I guess you're right. Thought they were bein' gallant or somethin', I guess."

"Yeah. I guess." Ignorant fools. Thought they could rescue the woman from the evil bandits. They'd bought into too many fairy stories, he reckoned. Brave knights and their ladies fair and all that nonsense.

And Tom was dead over it, as were a pair of men whose names he'd never learned. Somehow, this stung his conscience far worse than the life of the man he'd shot, the one who'd tried to run him down.

While he would never celebrate the man's death, Jed knew it had been a matter of shooting him or letting himself get trampled. Although he'd never much enjoyed the act of killing, it was in his nature to put his life above others.

He supposed, at the heart of things, that was in everyone's nature. Whether they cared to admit it or not.

The woman. Mrs. Furnish. It was because of her that this happened, her and the infernal code of chivalry some men refused to release even when those days were long over. It was a new world, especially once one stepped foot into Texas, and when one was dealing with armed bandits, one had best keep to themselves.

He cast a look over his shoulder and caught sight of Travis's slowing horse. "What happened to him?" Jed called out to Zeke.

"Him? Oh, I don't know. I don't think he got shot, but he hurt himself while fighting."

"He was fighting, too?" That was enough to make Jed pull the team to a stop and set the brake. "Did you look at it?"

"Didn't have time, did I?"

Jed scowled as he handed Zeke the reins and jumped from the wagon, going to where Travis had stopped the horse. "What happened to you? Can you ride?"

"I..." Travis winced, holding his arm with the other hand. "Might have dislocated the shoulder."

Jed swore a blue streak. Could any of them take care of themselves? While he'd more than understood the need to hasten from the area they'd committed the robbery, he wouldn't have forced his friend to ride for miles with a dislocated shoulder.

"Come on. Better let me set it back into place. I reckon this is as good a spot as any to set up camp for the night." He helped Travis from the horse and hobbled it before taking him to the wagon, where Mrs. Furnish glared at him from her place among their belongings.

It was a wonder she hadn't thrown or kicked them off while they rode. He'd have to thank his lucky stars for that and not give her chance to do so again.

"You gonna pop it in place?" Travis grimaced.

"Got to. You can't ride with that thing hanging useless. You need somethin' to bite down on?"

"Naw. Just get it over with." Travis turned his head away, leaning his bottom half against the wagon while Jed took his shoulder in one hand and his wrist in the other. He straightened Travis's arm slowly, regretting his friend's grunts of pain but knowing there was little to be done about it.

"One... two... three." On three, Jed jerked the arm upward in a quick, sharp thrust and felt the ball of the shoulder slide into the socket. Travis let out a single, anguished cry before going silent.

For some reason, rather than looking at his friend's face, he looked at the woman. Maybe he expected her to look green or even faint. Instead, she stared back at him with the calmest pair of eyes he'd ever seen.

So much so that for a split second, he thought she was dead—until she blinked.

"You've seen a man have his shoulder set before?" he asked.

"No."

"You've a strong constitution, then. That'll serve you well on the road."

She still appeared completely unmoved. What an unsettling woman. He turned his attention back to Travis, crafting a sling for him and tying it about his neck.

When that was done, he turned again to the blond-haired woman in the wagon. "All right, then, Mrs. Furnish. We'll be spending quite a lot of time together over these next weeks, so we might as well be friendly."

She raised a delicate eyebrow. "Friendly." It was not a question.

"Just like I said. There ain't no reason for you to get all uppity and shout and scream—if anything, it's only gonna make us mad, and that'll make things harder on you."

"While you're trying to be friendly."

He scowled. "What's so godawfully hard to understand about that?"

"You told me you had no such thing in mind, that's what's so hard to understand."

He blinked—then, he laughed when he caught her meaning. "For the sake of all that's holy, woman, you have a mighty high opinion of yourself."

"Or a low opinion of you," she hissed.

He brushed it off. This was to be expected. She wasn't going to offer to bake them a cake after getting kidnapped. "Either way, I didn't mean it the way you think I did. I meant real friendly, like people are when they're neighbors or just, you know, friends. Pleasant. Easy to get along with. Not fightin' like a cat in a washtub. Get my meaning now?"

She blinked slowly. "So you expect me to be your friend. Like we were neighbors. And not fight you after you stole me away from my coach." She spoke deliberately, like she was talking to a child.

"If you want this trip to go smooth, yeah. I do. At least, I hope you will. And we'll be nice, too. We're not a bad sort, really. We might look that way now, but you'll see."

"I doubt it." She turned her face away, the little, upturned nose that he would've found right cute on any other woman suddenly inspiring fury in him.

"Well, that's just fine, then. Acting like you're the Queen of England when you're dressed like a farmer's wife and travelin' on a stagecoach with almost a dozen people in all. Very fancy."

"At least I don't—" She didn't finish, cutting off so fast she might likely have bitten her tongue, but he got the idea. At least she didn't steal from people.

They were all alike, women such as her. Thinking they owned the world, that everybody who wasn't them was beneath them. Her husband might have dressed her like a poor little nobody to hide her in plain sight, but she was a stuck-up woman just the same.

A look over his shoulder told him Zeke had set up a fire for the night, as a chill had touched the air. The Yankee shivered but did not complain of the cold.

Even so, he couldn't have her freezing in the back of a wagon when he needed her healthy when he delivered her to Carson City.

"Come on, then. You might as well sleep near the fire." He leaned in, reaching for her.

She shimmied away.

He clenched his teeth against the flood of filth ready to pour out of his mouth. "Ma'am, I'm gonna give you til the count of three before I climb in there and fetch you myself."

"You wouldn't dare!" she spat as she crawled to the rear corner, furthest from him.

"Leave 'er alone, Jed," Zeke called out with a laugh in his voice. "Let 'er freeze her hide off."

This somehow managed to infuriate him further. Not only had Zeke used his name in front of the woman, he made a joke of what was a serious situation. If the woman wouldn't listen or obey orders, what were they going to do with her the entire long ride to Nevada?

He reached for her again and managed to grab an ankle. He used this to pull her to him while she wriggled and scurried and grunted from the effort of freeing herself. It was no use, of course, but she tried her hardest. By the time he pulled her all the way to the back end of the wagon, her hair had come undone from twisted braids on the back of her head and sweat beaded along her upper lip.

Damned if she wasn't just about the prettiest thing he'd ever seen up close, what with the way her cheeks flushed when she was in a rage, and her blue eyes flashed. Her lips parted so she might draw short, angry breaths, and he imagined her breathing that way beneath him...

It had been far too long since he'd been to a sporting house, indeed.

This thought went through his head at the very second the woman in his arms raised her knee and connected with that part of him that was beginning to stir against his wishes.

He groaned, pain exploding between his legs, the contents of his stomach threatening to let loose all over the woman's flower-printed dress as he fell against her for the briefest of moments. Tears squeezed from the corners of his eyes as he endured pain a woman would never understand.

And it was that pain that drew his arm back, hand raised, ready to slap her hard enough to turn her head around for what she'd done.

Only he'd never struck a woman before, and he wasn't about to just then. Pain or no pain. He stopped, hand still in the air, his teeth gritted and a snarl curling his upper lip.

He stopped and found she had not so much as flinched.

Why didn't she flinch? Or raise her arms to protect herself, or scream, or something?

She met his gaze head-on, clear and frank. Like she was daring him to do it. Like she wasn't the least bit scared.

His hand dropped to his side. "Who are you?" he breathed, still aching horribly and not just a little bitter, but more surprised by her than anything else.

She made no reply. He did not expect her to.

"Come." He did what he could to avoid limping as he led her the short distance to the fire, where Zeke and Travis made a clear point of avoiding his gaze. She arranged herself on the blanket Zeke had spread out, making a great deal of fuss over being unable to use her hands.

As if he cared just then, his private bits swollen and

aching as they were. If her damned hands fell off, it would serve her right.

He held onto that length of rope, though. Satan himself could not have convinced him to let go. He sat nearer the men, away from her—she rolled over, her back to them—and looked around.

"What do you make of that?" Travis asked, shaking his head with a smile which Jed knew belied his blank confusion.

"She didn't even flinch," Zeke marveled in a whisper.

What did Jed make of it? He had a few ideas, though they were nothing he wished to share with the others.

"C'mon," he said instead, gesturing to their blankets. "Better get some sleep. It's a long way to Carson City."

He, for one, was certain he wouldn't sleep a wink. Not with her over there, likely plotting a way to escape.

Not with the image of her unflinching face branded on his memory.

7

H ow dare he?

Of all the vile, contemptible pieces of trash, he was it. The very worst. They were terrible men, the other two, but he was the worst.

Jed. His name made her nose wrinkle in distaste as she remained with her back turned to them yet still connected to him by the rope he held. Would he ever let go that she might escape?

It mattered little. She could hardly run away while her hands were tied, could she? How would she manage to untie herself?

And what would she do even if she managed? Where was she? How would she get anywhere? On foot? It would take untold days, maybe, to arrive at a town or village. If she was lucky.

She might starve. She might fall prey to wolves or men even worse than the ones she was with.

She could not take that chance, especially with the baby in mind.

Not yet. Not until she was in better shape. Hands untied at least, able to mount a horse and ride away. She'd need to practice patience, then.

Patience? She knew all about patience. She'd been patient her entire life. Always waiting for something.

Waiting for her father to come back, when she hadn't understood how impossible that was. Waiting for John to finally show her kindness, which he never had.

Waiting for the tickets from Mark so she could finally make her escape.

She could wait a few more days, until Jed no longer felt she had to be tied—after all, he wanted to be her friend, didn't he? Friends did not leave each other tied at the wrist.

Memories of the men on the stage caused her to shift in place, uncomfortable. Her heart sank when she wondered who had been shot. The men were innocent. They didn't deserve it. These brutes thought they controlled who lived and who died, as if it was up to them.

Cowards. That was what they were. Men who could not face life honestly, who for some reason would not find gainful employment and would instead steal from others who'd earned what was theirs.

When she thought of what poor Mr. Lang would do without his beloved pocket watch. He was so clearly proud of it, always wiping away the smudges left by his finger-prints before returning it to his inside pocket.

And the man who'd sat beside her. A kind man whose

name she'd never gotten. Was he all right, or had they hurt him badly? Was he one of the men they'd shot? She doubted he would have tussled with a gunman—though there was no doubt of his courage, speaking out as he had, he did not strike her as a fool.

Only young, headstrong fools thought they would come out the better in a battle against rifles.

She jerked herself into a ball for protection, bringing her knees up and jerking on the rope some as she drew her hands to her chest.

The rope jerked back.

That insufferable man.

She jerked harder this time, her teeth set in determination.

He all but pulled her onto her back.

"Do you mind?" she hissed, rolling over to face him with hatred burning in her heart.

The smug grin he wore only served to deepen that hatred.

He held up his hand, the end of the rope in his fist. "Mind what? Making sure you don't jerk my arm clean off as I'm tryin' to get some shut-eye?"

"You could release the rope," she suggested in a whisper, aware of the other two men who appeared to be sleeping.

"Oh, yes. That would be just about the smartest move I ever made."

"I didn't mean untie me. I meant releasing the rope. I don't need you to hang onto it."

"This isn't about what you need. It's about what I need."

"Where do you think I'm going to go, hands bound as they are? I have no horse, no way to get anywhere and no way to free myself. And you took me away from the stage-coach without allowing me to bring my few things with me. I have nothing but the clothes on my back."

He gave a knowing smile. "Ah. So you've been thinking it over, I see."

Oh, damn him! Thinking he knew everything! She cursed him, as well as herself for blushing, and hoped the darkness covered it up.

He sat nearer the fire than she, and for once there was enough light to see his entire face by.

She cursed him again for being so handsome.

His dark brown hair waved gently down to his collar, thick and shining in the firelight. She'd imagined his mouth to be thin, but instead, it was full and well-shaped. Gray eyes stared at her from beneath thick brows, and when she did not look away a corner of that well-shaped mouth pulled up.

"Yes?" he challenged, raising his brows. "Do you have somethin' to say?"

"Nothing you'll want to hear."

"No, and you don't need to say a word," he smirked. She wished she could wipe it off his face. "The way you stare at me tells me you'd like to kill."

"I'm not like you. I don't kill." It came out as a growl, the faces of the men she'd only vaguely known flashing in front of her eyes as she spoke. She'd never know which of them had fallen. And there would likely be no justice for these outlaws.

If there was one thing she'd learned, it was the fickle nature of justice. Those who deserved it most hardly ever saw it.

He took this in and soon nodded. "No, I reckon you don't—but that doesn't mean you don't have it in you. If you could, you'd kill me right this very minute."

"You don't know me."

"I know killers. What else do I need to know?"

She sat up, leaned forward on her bound hands—they were fairly numb, but her arms could still support her. "You know nothing about me. You know nothing about what I've seen, what I've done. And yet I've still never fired a gun at an unarmed man with the intention of killing him."

"And I've only ever done it to protect myself." She scoffed. He glowered. "What's so funny about that?"

"Why should I believe you? You led an attack on a group of innocent people tonight."

"Nobody's innocent."

"Is that what you tell yourself? Does that make it easier to do what you do because you believe we're all guilty of something?"

His eyes narrowed to dangerous slits. Why was she pushing him this way? She'd never been so bold, not ever in her life. It was as though everything she'd ever held back —every tart word, every accusation she'd wished she could hurl at the men who visited her mother, at her husband— came rushing forth to be heard at last.

She held her breath, wondering if she'd finally gone too far. Waiting for what was surely to come. She'd endured physical pain before. If pain was the price to pay for speaking her mind, for finally having her say, that was the way it would simply have to be.

She would take her punishment and gladly if it meant setting him straight on who he truly was.

Yet instead of dragging her across the ground using that rope, instead of coming to her with a fist instead of an open hand this time, instead of instructing one of his men to deal with her, he merely picked up the hat he'd left by his side and rested it over his face, leaning back against his saddle as though going to sleep.

But he never let go of the rope.

The tension which had built over them popped like a soap bubble, leaving her somewhat breathless and unable to believe her nerve. She was fairly certain she'd won something. A battle without a name.

When she lay down again, she was smiling in relief, in disbelief. She had spoken her mind and had not suffered punishment.

Yet.

Her smile disappeared.

He might have punishment in mind for her. They would be together a long time—much longer than she wished, naturally, but especially with her condition, as it was and her haste to arrive in Carson City.

What would he do? Would her daring seem worthwhile then?

Exhaustion got the better of her before she could grasp and hold onto the image of his pained, enraged expression as he'd pulled back to strike her—before she had time to remind herself that he had not struck when he might have. That he had held himself back.

8

"Can you feel it?"

Travis did not need to tell Jed what "it" was. The sizzle in the air. There were moments when he was unable to take an easy breath.

"Yeah, I do," he grunted. "Sky's gonna light up today. Sooner rather than later."

The three of them met up in the center of the camp they had just taken down, looking at one another for some clue of what to do next. It still felt unnatural for Tom to be missing.

And they'd left his body lying out there, in the middle of nowhere. That would stick with him forever, another sin for him to carry. One of so many.

"What'll we do?" Zeke asked, rubbing the back of his neck as he liked to do when he was at a loss. "We take off now, we might get caught up in it. We stick around…"

He didn't need to finish. They couldn't afford to hang

back for even a half a day, being so close to the scene of the robbery. Lawmen would ride out in all directions, covering miles at a stretch.

But a storm would keep them inside, too. Nobody familiar with riding out in the middle of open land took a chance during a lightning storm. Jed could still vividly remember stories of men who'd dared it and wound up fried to a crisp.

He looked at the woman, where she sat in the wagon. What had he been thinking, taking her? Sure, he wanted the money. Needed it. But she was a pain in the neck he'd rather not suffer. Her stare was heavy, expectant.

"I say we start movin', then stop the minute we see the first bolt. I don't wanna take chances, but I don't wanna take the chance of hanging around and gettin' ourselves found here, either."

"Sounds right to me," Travis agreed. He'd be riding beside Jed in the wagon, his wounded shoulder still too tender to allow for decent riding. Zeke mounted up, and they started out.

She'd been quiet all through the morning, not saying a word even to protest Jed guarding her while she squatted behind a bush. He hadn't watched, of course—that was never his predilection—but she hadn't raised a fuss. Hadn't even shot him a filthy look, which she was so good at.

What was she planning? There had to be something on her mind.

As if he needed something else to worry about.

Ominous clouds rolled in from the west, coloring the

already gray sky a deeper shade. The hair on the back of Jed's neck stood up from the charge in the air. He laid the reins to the backs of the team, spurring them on to greater speed. They needed to cover some ground, any ground, before there came time to stop.

A glance over his shoulder told him Mrs. Furnish rode with her back to him, staring out at the land they left behind. What a strange woman. Strange and frustrating as hell.

If she screamed and carried on, he would deal with that. He expected it. Yes, he'd warned her against it, but he hadn't expected the woman to listen.

Something told him he would rarely get what he expected from her.

"You all right back there?" he asked. For some reason, he couldn't let her be. Maybe because she wouldn't let him be, taking over his thoughts as she did.

"Yes."

That was it. One single word.

Travis chuckled, which told Jed he needed to hide his frustration better. He didn't need everyone knowing the way the woman got under his skin. It was weakness, and while he didn't mind the occasional joke made at his expense, this was something else entirely.

Besides, she might overhear their joking, and he didn't need her getting ideas.

"How much you think we ought to ask for her?" Travis asked in a low voice.

Jed thought this over, doing some quick sums in his

head. Sums were always something he'd been good at. He didn't even need a pencil and paper to add up long columns of figures.

Land was around five dollars an acre, and he'd want around five hundred. Nothing too much—he wasn't trying to start at the top. Ten acres per head would leave him at fifty head of cattle, to begin with. He'd need supplies to build him a cabin, equipment...

And this was just for him. What about Travis and Zeke?

Damn it all. He hadn't thought about that. He couldn't ask for one figure for himself and another for the other two. Anything they received would have to be split three ways. So whatever he needed, he'd have to multiply by three.

Would Furnish be willing to pay such an amount?

What if he started out smaller and only purchased the land? Or if he purchased less land and fewer head of cattle?

Another glance over his shoulder. Would she know how much money her husband would be able to get his hands on in a short amount of time? While Jed was not a wealthy man and while he hadn't been on a working ranch in over ten years, he knew much of a rancher's wealth was tied up in his land, his stock. He didn't have it lying around in bags in a bank, or in a safe in his home.

He might be able to ask her if he could only warm her up a bit. That holier-than-thou attitude of hers was a real problem. She'd have to start being human and stop looking down on them.

On him, in particular. Zeke and Travis didn't exactly have a way with women, and not because neither of them was particularly easy on the eyes. They were about as gentle and understanding as a pair of bulls—the sorts of gals working in the sporting houses were all they were fit for. Women who didn't expect a man to have manners. Just money.

He, on the other hand, could at least put on an air of gentility if he needed to. He'd witnessed it enough as a boy —the deference, the chivalrous behavior. It had been a lot of years since he'd spent a decent stretch of time with a woman, having been in the presence of men the rest of it. His skills would be a bit rusty, what skills there were.

All he could do was try.

And he thought he knew where to start once clouds of an even more ominous nature began piling up in the distance. Unlike those already spanning the sky, these were greenish. A bad sign.

"We'd better see about finding cover," he announced, then over his shoulder, "You needn't worry. We'll get under shelter as soon as we can."

Travis shot him a questioning look, but fortunately kept his mouth shut. This was not the time for questions.

"We can set up the tent wherever we go," he decided, the horses now running at a moderate pace as Jed strove to outrun the storm. It looked to be a bad one—already a cool wind moved across his overheated skin, telling him of the threat of hail from those clouds. "That'll be good for her."

"Her? What about us?" Travis asked.

Jed shot him a warning look. Just when he'd been sure his partner would stay quiet. "You and Zeke can cover up the wagon and huddle inside or even underneath for all I care."

"And you?"

Jed glared at him as long as he dared before turning his attention to the team and whether they remained on a straight course. The weather had them riled up, too.

It was as if the presence of a woman had turned his partners stupid—Tom, too, for that matter, as he'd allowed himself to be disarmed. That meant his guard had been down. Damned fool might as well have asked to get shot with his own gun.

"I'll be in the tent," he muttered through clenched teeth, hoping his voice was low enough that she might not hear and protest.

Travis's lopsided mouth grew even more so when he snickered, but Jed took care to maintain a serious expression. He would not be in there for pleasurable reasons. He'd never forced himself on a woman and never would, by God.

His longtime friend and partner should have known him better than that.

A bolt of lightning zigzagged to the ground, coming from those dark green clouds. He stopped caring whether Travis thought him capable of raping a woman and focused himself on getting them safe.

It wouldn't matter who rode out the storm in the tent with her if they never got the chance to set one up.

Zeke had a hell of a challenge getting his horse to obey commands, and the team was starting to spook a little too much for Jed's liking. They wanted nothing more than to bolt, which meant his arms and shoulders were taking a beating as he struggled to control them.

"We gotta stop," he decided.

Zeke pointed to a group of boulders away off, and Jed nodded in agreement, taking the team off the road and into the brush. The wagon bounced horribly, but Jed couldn't look back to be certain the Yankee was safe.

Until they came to a stop and he set the brake, then turned.

To find the wagon empty save their supplies.

"Damn it!" He stood, his head turning this way and that. How long ago had she jumped? For she would not have fallen out. She would have risked her fool neck by jumping.

How he knew, he couldn't have said. She seemed the type, was all.

"Mrs. Furnish!" he shouted, hands cupped around his mouth. "Mrs. Furnish!"

No answer, not that he expected one. He turned to Zeke. "Set up the tent, get the team unhitched." He mounted the horse Zeke had only just hobbled.

"What are you doing?" Travis shouted as Jed rode away.

Acting like a damned fool, that was what he was doing. Looking for a woman more trouble than she was worth. Just this alone, chasing her down as she risked both their lives, ought to earn him a solid ten thousand dollars.

Furnish had to know what a godawful pain the woman was, what they would go through to get her to Carson City. He doubted she was a wilting flower at home, blushing and staying silent whenever the menfolk were around.

Lightning flashed, again, the bolts touching the ground and leaving Jed's heart racing the same as the horse's hooves against the ground.

"Mrs. Furnish!" he called out, his eyes sweeping the area. Damn the woman. Where did she think she was going to go with her hands bound?

And damn him forever for leaving her a little slack that morning while binding them together. He'd wanted to take it easier on her once he'd gotten a look at the chafing the rope had caused. She might have freed herself.

Thunder cracked the sky wide open, and with it came the rain. The horse reared, his head all but split from the earth-shaking rumble.

"Mrs. Furnish!" He pulled the brim of his hat lower to block some of the rain from his eyes, but it was little help once the downpour soaked through.

One more try, and then he'd have to consider his unworthy hide. He pulled in a deep lungful of air and nearly screamed to be heard over the roaring rain. "I can leave you out here in this, or I can take you to shelter! It's up to you!" Thunder cracked as if he'd planned it so.

That was when he caught sight of a white calico dress, a sodden bonnet, the figure wearing both bobbing up and down as she ran away from him.

"Son of a..." He took off after her in spite of the horse's reluctance to do so. He couldn't blame it. Maybe the beast was smarter than he was.

It took little effort to catch up to the woman, running in the rain, her dress soaked through and probably slowing her down. She didn't wear the hoops women used to wear before the war—sometimes he'd wondered how they managed to make it through the door in those contraptions—so the skirts hung heavy around her, though she gathered them up around her legs.

"What do you think you're doing?" he shouted once he caught up.

Sure enough, she had untied the rope, and from the way she limped, she'd had a rough landing from the back of the wagon.

It served her right.

"No! No!" She fought like a wildcat as he hauled her up onto the saddle, biting his arm at one point.

He howled and again nearly struck her for it but held himself back.

He'd be lucky if he made it out of this alive at the rate she was going, kicking and biting and dragging him further out into a thunderstorm.

"Do you wanna get yourself fried out here? Or maybe you wanna drown!"

His horse needed no urging to hurry it the hell away from there.

"Well, let me tell you somethin'," he barked into her ear as they rode. "I took you last night, and you're my responsibility. I'm not gonna let you get your fool self killed out here."

"Let me go!" She elbowed him in the stomach and damn near shoved him from the saddle.

"I will take you with me!" he snarled, his voice sharp enough to make her cringe. That seemed to take the fight out of her and thank God for it. By the time they reached the sight where Zeke and Travis waited, the tent was set up, and the two of them were huddled under the wagon.

Jed was less kind than he'd been before when he pulled the woman from the saddle and shoved her into the tent with a warning to stay put. He saw to the horse's relative comfort, wincing whenever thunder rattled the ground.

After that, there was nothing to do but join her inside.

He'd asked for this, hadn't he?

9

I n spite of the warmth in the air, she shivered hard enough to rattle her teeth. Soaked calico hung all around her, sticking to her skin just the way her hair and bonnet did.

She'd been less comfortable, though it was difficult to remember when.

And he would be back for her. No way he'd let her out of his sight ever again. She had ruined any chance of getting away, and all because she hadn't been able to run fast enough with all that heavy calico in her hands.

He barged into the tent before she had the chance to do any more thinking. "What are you tryin' to do? Break your neck? Do you really think we would hurt you? Is it that important to get away?"

He reminded her of how she used to scold the boys when they got into dangerous mischief.

There was nothing for her to say at first, as the sight of him took her breath away.

This was new.

She'd never had her breath taken away at the sight of a man. Not even the first time she'd laid eyes on John. For all his many faults, he was a good-looking man, tall and broad and dark of hair and eyes.

But she'd never had this fluttery, breathless feeling before. Like a whole jar full of butterflies was emptied into her stomach and flew around.

His shirt, a tan color when dry, was soaked through and stuck to him as her dress did to her. Every muscle of his shoulders, his arms, chest, and stomach were as clear as they would've been had he taken the thing off. And a life spent riding horses and living outdoors showed on his chiseled body.

"Didn't you hear me?" he demanded, ripping off his dripping hat and throwing it to the ground.

"I did," she whispered, teeth still chattering, eyes stuck on his now nearly black hair, dripping water onto his shoulders, down his neck. What would it be like to touch his skin the way those droplets did?

What a disturbing thought!

He stared at her for a moment, then sighed and swore under his breath. He passed where she sat on the cot one of the other men had set up—the tent was large enough to hold them both comfortably, hardly smaller than the tarpaper shack in which she'd grown up—and pulled out a blanket to wrap around her shoulders.

"I didn't jump out," she breathed, glaring up at him. "I didn't. I was bounced out."

He stared down at her, his brows drawn together, as though deciding whether or not she meant it.

She did. If he knew about the child she carried inside, she could have used that as a means to prove her honesty. Never would she have leaped from a moving wagon when it could have meant the child's life.

"I fell out," she insisted. "If my hands had been free, I might have held on. There was no way to do so. I slid out of the back and onto the ground. I even cried out, but you didn't hear me."

He blinked, the lines between his brows relaxing. "Is that true?"

"It is." That first moment, hitting the ground. Curled in a ball, every instinct telling her to protect her belly. Whether it had done any good remained to be seen. She'd managed to scramble away, unravel the knot in the ropes with her teeth and run without suffering any cramping, but there was no telling.

What would happen if she lost the child while she was with these men? She might die, too. They wouldn't know how to take care of her.

"Why did you try to run away when I came after you? You must have heard me screaming for you, yet I found you running away."

She looked at her shoes, now mud-covered. "I had to try."

To her surprise, it sounded like he laughed. When she looked up, he was smiling.

"I'll give you that one," he said as he crouched beside her. "Just do me the favor of never tryin' that again, all right? I'm pleading with you here, and I don't plead easily."

"I told you, I didn't try."

He sighed with impatience. "Running, I mean. I need you not to run."

She looked down again, this time to avoid his eyes. His deep, deep eyes. She'd never seen eyes like them, the color of steel or a stormy sky.

When she looked into them, that fluttery feeling came back, and she didn't know what to do with that.

"I need to get to Carson City, Jed." Maybe if she used his name, he would feel closer to her. He would be kinder to her. "It is so important that I get there as soon as possible."

"Why? What's the emergency?"

She shook her head. "You don't need to know that. I don't ask you about your business, do I?"

"No, but you have opinions about it just the same."

Her head snapped up, eyes meeting his again. This time, there was no breathless fluttering. It was more like she'd swallowed fire. "When a group of men kidnap you while holding guns, tell me how it makes you feel. Tell me how hard you try to escape. You know you would never stop trying. Even I know that, and I hardly know you at all."

The only sound for a long time was that of the wind and rain beating against the canvas walls of the tent.

"You're right. You hardly know me at all." He stood,

hands on his slim hips. He had large hands, strong hands. Hands that could span her waist from the back of a horse and lift her as though she weighed nothing more than a feather.

He was too distracting.

"You hardly know me," he repeated, "but you call me names, you say things about what I do. You decided who I was last night, and you treat me like the man you think I am."

Just like a man. Turning things around, making it her fault. "I don't have to like you any more than you have to like me. We are not friends. We do not have to be friendly. I want you to get me to Carson City, to my husband, and I want us to move quickly."

He scoffed.

She reminded him, "The sooner we get there, the sooner you get the money you're so desperate to get."

He turned away, cursing again. She folded her arms, staring straight ahead.

It didn't matter that he was the only man who'd ever stirred her blood the way he did. He was a murderer. She'd had enough of men like him to last her a lifetime.

The ground shook when thunder rolled through, making her tremble again and even whimper softly like a wounded puppy. She hated thunder even more than she hated John Carter. Even more than she hated the man standing in front of her.

"Are you all right?" he muttered.

"Fine," she spat.

"You don't sound fine. You sound scared."

"I said I was fine." And she was. She truly was. Deep breaths, in and out, and she would be fine. Thunder never hurt anybody, and she was safe from the lightning and rain and even the wind. Nothing could hurt her.

He turned, taking a knee at her side. "Did you hurt yourself when you fell from the wagon?"

She shook her head. "Nothing I can't handle. Thank you." It came out stiff, formal.

"Nothing you can't handle?"

She didn't reply.

"You've handled a lot of injuries, then?"

She gave him a withering look which she hoped conveyed nothing but disgust—and hid that fluttering he stirred up. "I thought we talked about staying out of each other's business."

He studied her, his eyes narrowing as they flicked over her face. "What happened to you? Why didn't you flinch when I made like I was gonna hit you?"

She should have known he would ask, as her reaction had unsettled him so. What would he say if he knew how many blows she had endured? "I don't flinch."

"Why not? Are you used to getting hit?"

"I don't want to talk about this."

"Does Furnish beat you? Mark Furnish, the great rancher?"

"I said I don't want to talk about it!" He blinked hard, pulling back when she shouted in his face. Shame flushed her cheeks—didn't she know all too well how it felt when someone shouted in her face?

Modulating her tone, she continued, "Not him. Not Mark. He's never laid a hand on me."

This was true. Not so much as a finger. Not even his eyes. She could at least rest easy in that.

His face softened. "But somebody has."

When his hand touched hers, she wasn't sure what to do. Pull away? Slap his face for taking liberties? Allow him to hold it?

There didn't seem to be the need to slap him or even to take offense at the brief intimacy. For he was gentle, far more so than she would've guessed he was capable of.

No one had ever touched her gently before—and it was the knowing of it, much more than the memory of violence, which brought tears to her eyes.

"That is the past," she assured him. "A long time ago." Who was she trying to convince? Herself?

For it was not a long time ago. It was a matter of mere weeks. Only weeks since the last time he'd struck her, sneering down at her as she'd curled into a protective ball on the kitchen floor.

No wonder she had curled into that same ball upon falling from the wagon. It was second nature by then.

Jed looked down, seemed surprised at the fact that her hand was still in his. He was quick to withdraw his fingers. To her surprise, she mourned the loss of his touch.

"I could make a deal with you."

"A deal?"

"I promise to make sure the other men are kind to you, that they're never rough with their words or their manners. But you've gotta promise me to behave yourself, too. You say you're in a hurry to get someplace, but if you try to run it'll only slow us down."

She saw the sense in this. And, truly, if she ran, it would only endanger two lives.

"Do not bind my hands again," she countered, seeing her opportunity in the way he'd softened in manner.

Just like that, he hardened again. She should have known.

"I can't promise you that," he muttered, his eyes darkening with foreboding.

"Then, I won't promise not to try to get away. If you treat me like a captive, I'll only spend my time thinking of ways to free myself. And I will not be pleasant."

"We can be more unpleasant," he warned.

"We'd have to see about that." Her eyes darted down to the place she'd kicked the night before—not long, for that would be immodest, and she already felt a tingle in the back of her neck at the thought of him—then back up to his face. "I was pretty unpleasant to you last night, wasn't I?"

He looked away, but not soon enough for her to miss the way he grimaced. "That's a word for it."

"Remember, I could have held on inside the wagon if my hands were free."

He stood, shaking his head. "Damn it all, woman. Why can't anything be easy with you?"

She gritted her teeth. "I never asked you to take me along, remember. I don't have to make things easy. This was your decision, and you have to live with it. The sooner you get me home, the sooner you won't have to deal with me."

The storm had let up, she realized, when they fell silent. Typical of spring and summer storms, quick to flare up and then die out.

Jed went to the flap, pulling it back to look outside. Tension made itself known in every line of his body, from his raised shoulders to the way his hands fisted around the canvas tight enough for his knuckles to go bone white.

He turned his face that she might see his finely carved profile. It seemed wrong, somehow, for a man so handsome to be engaged in such filthy business.

"I won't tie your hands anymore. But so help me, if you get it into your head to act foolish, it won't be me you deal with. It'll be them. And if you think I'm some terrible thing, remember that I'm not the one who shot those men from the coach last night. I only shot at the one trying to run me down, Mrs. Furnish."

The way he said that name. So much bitterness.

"Melissa. Call me Melissa, please." Not only because she had no right to the name Furnish, but because she couldn't stand hearing him snarl it as he did.

The sound of the tent flap's closing behind him may as well have been the slamming of a door.

10

"How do you expect me to wash myself while you are nearby?"

She marched up from the river, through the brush between it and the place where they'd set up camp the night before. Her tiny hands were curled into fists, swinging at her sides.

Jed bit the side of his tongue to keep from falling into another argument with her. She loved to get his blood up and had been doing so all through Colorado. Pity the man who lived with her; no wonder her husband had let her go across the country on her own.

If Jed were in his shoes, he wouldn't be in any hurry to get her back.

"You seem to have done a good enough job of it even so, and it isn't like I was watching. I had my back to you the whole time," he reminded her when they came to a stop, letting his eyes roam over her wet hair, her fresh-scrubbed cheeks. Cheeks which turned pink under the weight of gaze, just as he'd known they would.

She turned away. "I would like to use the privacy of the tent to comb and dress my hair, if you don't mind."

"Fine with me. Just don't think you can stay in there all day. We'll be headin' out soon." He got a tent flap thrown shut in his face, and he grinned.

Sometimes it was a struggle to know whether he wished to kiss her or spank her like a naughty child. He could just imagine her on a ranch, standing at the head of the table while the hands ate their midday meal, telling them to mind their manners and asking if they wanted seconds. As his mother had done so many times.

He could imagine her henpecking a man to death, too. Just as his mother had nearly done to his father.

He turned away from the tent, as though this would help him get away from the memory.

Travis was tending the horses while Zeke went to the river for a wash-up before they left. It would be another few days before they made it out of Colorado before heading into Utah Territory on the way to Nevada.

Such a long journey. Dangerous, too, with all sorts of unnamed challenges out there—not the least of which were Indians.

But he believed, somehow, that the Yankee in the tent could handle herself. He almost felt sorry for the brave who tried to take her for a squaw.

Though he would never allow that to happen. He might

have taken her so he could profit, but she was his responsibility until the minute he handed her over.

They'd been lucky enough so far to avoid anything more dangerous than a few coyotes, snakes and the like. The sorts of things a man was accustomed to after riding the plains for years.

If anything, the woman was the most dangerous thing of all.

Travis and Zeke avoided her like the plague, and he didn't think she took it too hard. In fact, she seemed to prefer not talking to them very much outside of the necessities. Not that she spoke very much to him, either, outside of pestering him.

If he made it out of this without the woman nagging him to death, it would be nothing short of a miracle.

"Daggum it!"

Jed's head snapped up at the sound of Zeke's shouts from the river. Melissa ducked out of the tent, one hand over her heart.

"You stay put or else risk getting lost out here," he ordered, leaving her unguarded in favor of running through the waist-high brush to where Zeke sat, clutching his ankle at the water's edge.

"I think... a snake..." Zeke's face contorted in a grimace.

"Lemme see." He eased his friend's hand from the ankle, and sure enough, a pair of pinpoints sat in the center of an area that was quickly starting to swell.

The last thing any of them needed. The very last thing.

He pushed back the rush of dismay which rose in his chest, favoring action instead. He began working at his belt, sliding it through the loops in his trousers, wrapping it low down on Zeke's leg and cinching it tightly above the wound.

"Yeah, looks like you attracted a friend there in the water," he observed while he worked, chuckling in spite of the dryness in his mouth.

The attempt at humor fell flat. "I'm done for, ain't I?"

Jed met his friend's eyes, and he saw the blank terror in them. "Not if I have anything to say about it. Did you see anything? Do you know what kind it was?"

Zeke shook his head.

"I need you to calm down. Make yourself do it. Breathe slowly. In. Out." The greater Zeke's panic, the faster the poison would work its way into his system. Already, the swelling was beginning to worsen. Jake hoped to at least hold back the progression with the belt, but that wouldn't last forever.

He helped Zeke to his feet and called out for Travis, who came on the run. "Snakebite," he muttered, and that was all he had to say. Travis ran ahead to build a fire where they had only just put one out.

Melissa watched, wide-eyed, as Travis helped Zeke lie down on a blanket in front of the wood Travis stacked. Flames flickered there moments later.

Jed pulled out his knife, trying in vain to joke and keep the mood light as he held the blade over the fire. "You know what I have to do," he murmured, meeting Zeke's gaze from the corner of his eye.

"Yeah, I reckon I do." Sweat poured from Zeke's brow. "Damn it, it hurts."

"I'm sorry for that. It's gonna hurt worse before it gets better." He caught Travis's eye. "Mix me up some mud."

"Is there anything I can do?" Melissa asked as Travis ran back to the river.

"You can sit down and stay out of the way and not bother me," Jed replied, not bothering to look up. He cared little for what she thought just then, for whether his words landed too harshly. She was not his concern.

All of his attention needed to be on what he was about to do.

He pulled Zeke's flask from his boot, still sitting where he'd left it before going down for a bath. It was half-full. "Here. Drink your fill but leave just a bit for your leg."

Zeke tipped the thing back, his throat working as he swallowed as much whiskey as he could hold. When there was nothing but a splash left, he handed it to Jed who poured it over the wound to clean the skin.

"Ahh, damn it all!" Zeke grunted, squeezing his eyes shut.

"And to think, I haven't touched blade to skin yet." He waved the knife around a bit to cool it before use. "All right, now. You know what I'm gonna do."

"Just do it fast," Zeke implored.

"I would look away, Mrs. Furnish," Jed announced before bringing the knife down, slicing a line down the length of the swollen flesh.

Zeke jumped, tendons standing out on the side of his

thick neck. Travis returned with a bowl full of mud, just in time to help hold Zeke down while Jed squeezed out the blood and fluid which had already begun to build up.

It might have been too late. There was no way to tell until the sickness worked its way through him. Jed used all the pressure he could to squeeze the wound until there was no longer swelling or built-up fluid, then poured water from one of the canteens over it to wash away the mess.

"It's hot," Zeke panted.

"I know." Jed wrapped a kerchief around the wound and tied it tight before smearing mud over the top to cool the hot, soon-to-be-burning patch of flesh. "You'd best empty this canteen into your belly now and be ready for me to force more of it down your throat, even when you don't want to drink anymore."

He would need all the water his body could hold once the sweating started, but he'd also more than likely vomit which would empty him out. It would be a fine line to walk, one which would stretch on for days.

Looking up from Zeke meant meeting Melissa's troubled gaze. She saw this for what it was, as he did.

There was a chance she'd be watching a man die before long.

Jed splashed his face in the water Travis brought from the river. He didn't dare leave Zeke long enough to go down for a bath—not that he didn't trust Travis, but he preferred to manage such tasks on his own.

He did not think Travis minded a bit, that he was, in fact, more than happy to allow Jed the responsibility of cleaning up after their sick friend.

And Zeke was sick. Terribly so. He'd gone through the teeth-chattering chills, the shouts of pain as his leg burned like it was on fire—his words. He'd wept, he'd even prayed. Prayed for salvation. Prayed for death.

Jed had sat through it all.

So had Melissa.

The first night, he'd pulled her aside. Zeke was asleep, shifting fretfully but asleep. "I need to know something," Jed had muttered, turning his full attention to her for the first time since the snakebite.

"What is it? If you're asking whether I know about snakebites, the answer is no."

If she'd spoken with so much as a hint of that nasty, highfalutin attitude of hers, he might have broken his rule of never striking a woman. At that point, his nerves were far too frayed to bother himself with a code of conduct.

Instead, she'd answered with a hint of concern. She wished to help, he realized, but did not know how.

He'd softened somewhat, his shoulders falling back to their normal place. They had been up around his ears before then. "I need to know if I can trust you to help me if the time comes. I might need your help with him—he's a big man, and he's bound to get pretty ornery once the fever sets in and he doesn't know where he is. I expect Travis, and I can hold him down, but you might have to be the one to help clean the wound while we do."

She'd taken this in with no surprise at all. In fact, he had wondered at first if he should repeat his instructions, if she had understood him.

"You can trust me." It was all she'd said, and all she'd needed to say.

And up to that point, he had trusted her. She'd gone to fetch water, she'd helped clean Zeke up when he got sick all over himself. She'd washed his clothes in the river and mopped the sweat off his forehead.

She'd even insisted he sleep in the tent while she spent her night either by his side or out in the open, as he needed shelter from the sun and any pests flying around.

For two days, she had worked just as hard as Jed had while Travis saw to fixing the food and tending the horses. Whether she did it to gain favor, or because she was a decent woman, Jed couldn't say and did not possess the strength to work out.

He did not even have it in him to speak with her except about Zeke. How he appeared to be faring, whether he'd woken up while either Jed or Melissa were sleeping, whether he'd been able to hold down any food.

He had not, up to that point, on the morning of the third day after the bite.

The tent reeked of vomit, excrement, and sour sweat. Jed knew this, but the stench hardly registered on him any longer when he stepped inside.

Zeke was exactly where he'd spent three days—in the

cot. Except now, his eyes were open and staring blankly up at the canvas overhead.

Jed's heart seized. It was over. Zeke was dead.

Then, his friend's chest rose as he drew a breath.

To his surprise and shame, Jed found himself torn between relief and disappointment. For Zeke had suffered terribly and would continue to do so until his fever broke— or he died. In the brief moment when Jed had thought him dead, the idea of his friend being out of pain had felt like a blessing.

Melissa had fallen asleep beside the cot, her head resting against the wooden frame near Zeke's knee. In sleep, her face fell into peaceful lines. Her youth struck him for the first time—he'd thought her older, perhaps in her middle twenties, but just then she might have been eighteen, with strands of golden hair brushing her cheek.

The impulse to tuck them behind her ear, maybe letting his fingers trail over her cheekbone, the curve of her ear, the slope of her neck, was yet another surprise. Though he felt no shame this time.

Instead of touching her in that intimate way, he nudged her shoulder in passing while going to check on his friend. It was the most he trusted himself to touch her without taking liberties he ought not to take.

She stirred to wakefulness as he bent over Zeke. "Good morning," he grinned. "You decided to spend a little time awake today."

He looked terrible, his skin gray, sweat turning his reddish hair nearly brown. His eyes had a sunken look, with dark circles beneath. His lips were dry, cracked, for no matter how they tried to keep fluids in him they simply came back out.

As though she read his mind, Melissa dipped a cloth into a bucket of water and squeezed it over his mouth before mopping the sweat.

"Jed?" Zeke's voice, normally so loud, so strident, reminded Jed of a frightened child.

"I'm here." He patted Zeke's shoulder.

"I... saw..." He drew a shallow breath. "My... mama was here..."

Jed clenched his teeth at this, his brow furrowing. Melissa looked up at him with a question in her wide, blue eyes. He shook his head only once, which sent the message —Zeke's mother had passed away when he was no older than thirteen.

A frown touched her full mouth, and when she looked down at Zeke, there was nothing but pity in her gaze.

She drew a deep breath, stroking his brow all the while with the cool cloth. "Did she speak to you?"

"No, I don't think so," he whispered. "She just smiled at me so... like she used to. When I was a boy."

"I bet that was real nice, seeing her." Melissa's voice was low, calm, soothing. She might as well have been talking to a baby, easing it into sleep.

"It was... Made me feel good..."

"After being so sick, I'm glad you felt good." She lowered the sheet covering him from the shoulders down, wiping his neck and chest in smooth, slow strokes, humming softly as she did.

Jed could only stand back and watch. It seemed as though she ought not to be disturbed.

"Hurts. Hurts everywhere…"

"I know, I know," she crooned. "I know it hurts. It won't hurt much longer."

"Promise?" He looked at her for the first time, his eyes no longer glassy with fever. Instead, they were wet with unshed tears.

"I promise." She placed his hands on his chest, patting them.

"Jed?" Zeke looked about himself until he landed on Jed's face.

"I'm here." He patted Zeke's shoulder again.

"What happens… everything I done…"

Jed winced. "I don't know. I suspect if you're real sorry for hurting anybody you might've hurt, there's forgiveness."

"What about the other things?"

Jed chuckled. "Things we ought not talk about in front of a lady?" Was he truly chuckling while at his partner's deathbed? Unthinkable.

And more than that, she chuckled, too. "You might be surprised what I've heard in my day. Things that might make even you blush."

Zeke's soft laugh was familiar, carefree, the one Jed remembered.

Then, it faded. And he was gone.

11

Melissa sat back on her calves, the air suddenly still.

As a grave.

In all her years, with everything she'd seen and done and suffered, she had never eased a man into death.

This was not a good man. She'd worked to save him for the better part of three days knowing all the while that he was not good. He robbed people, used force, threatened and shot them.

And yet she'd done it, even though he had never been kind to her.

She hadn't had the time or strength to ask herself why at the time, as she wiped up his mess and checked for fever and did everything she could to ease his pain.

Now that he was gone and there was nothing more to do for him, she could not understand why she'd gone to the trouble. Maybe because there was nothing else to do? Or because she was never one to sit idly by when others struggled?

Perhaps because he was a human being, like herself. One who'd seen visions of his dead mother, who wept when he considered the evil he'd done in his life and questioned whether he'd be punished for it.

He ought to have done a bit more thinking on the matter before then, she thought.

Jed, meanwhile, let out a long breath. He had not moved from the head of the cot, though there was nothing left in it but a shell that was once a person.

She chewed her lip, wondering what to say now. Condolences seemed appropriate. "I am sorry," she whispered, looking down at the hands she'd folded in her lap. "You did everything you could. You worked very hard to save his life."

"Why did you?"

The response surprised her. It seemed out of place considering what they'd just been through. In fact, up until that very moment, before he took such a harsh tone, she had started to warm to him. There had to be a depth of good in a man willing to work night and day to save another man's life.

In comparison, their friend Travis might just as well have been a stranger.

She looked up to find him studying her, one eyebrow raised.

"Well? Why did you do work so hard?"

Could he know she had only just been asking the same

of herself? Impossible, though it was an odd coincidence, him bringing it up when he did. "I don't know."

He snorted. "Are you always so honest?"

"Not always." Sometimes not at all. "He was a person, same as you or me or anybody. He was in pain. And..."

She turned away, back to Zeke's body. And she'd felt sorry for Jed, knowing he would have to take the entire burden of caring for an injured man on himself. Was that truly why she'd done it? To help him? Him?

He was either too heartsick or too tired to press her for more. "We'll have to bury him soon," Jed observed, drawing the back of his arm over his forehead. "It'll be a hot one today."

Yes, there was already sweat running down her back.

She left the tent with a heavy heart but was glad for a bit of fresh air after breathing in so much staleness and sickness.

The click of a cocked pistol froze her heart. She looked straight ahead to find the muzzle pointed directly between her eyes.

"You're bad luck," Travis whispered. "This is your fault."

Her mouth went dry. Words ceased to form in her head.

"Travis," Jed spoke up, behind her. She thanked God he'd come out when he did. He might be able to talk sense to the fool.

"This is her. Don't you see?" Travis's eyes shifted away from Melissa to a spot over her right shoulder. "First Tom gets shot, then Zeke gets bit. And now he's dead, I was standin' outside and heard everything. He's gone now, and this is all because of her."

"She didn't do anything," Jed reminded him in a tone not unlike the one she'd used when she was speaking to Zeke in his final minutes. Cool, calm, soothing. "And if she did, it's my fault. It was my idea to bring her along. So if you're gonna blame anybody for what's happenin' to us, blame me. Take it out on me. Not on her."

Jed moved her aside and stepped forward, standing straight in front of the pistol. "Go on, then. Shoot, if you're gonna."

She couldn't breathe. Was this truly happening? Would the horrors of this day ever end?

Travis licked his lips, holding the pistol steady. "I don't wanna do this to you."

"And I don't want you to," Jed admitted, "but you're the one who seems all hell-bent on makin' somebody pay. If you're gonna, then do it. I understand what it's like to want justice done, believe me. If this is what's gonna make it right for you, by all means."

The two of them stared at each other while Melissa debated running. The desire to protect herself and her baby was most pressing, but if she ran, Travis might shoot. Besides, she was not entirely sure she could move if she tried.

Finally, the gun began to lower. "I want outta here," Travis announced. "I don't wanna wait around until it's my turn to have somethin' happen."

"That's your right. You're a free man." Jed stood still,

watching as Travis released the hammer and slid the pistol into its holster.

"If you're smart, you'll get rid of her." Travis cast a hateful eye her way. He could look at her any way he wanted, so long as he did not shoot.

They watched as he mounted his horse—he'd already packed his things, Melissa noted—and took off north.

"That was unfortunate, and I am sorry he did it." Jed did not look at her, but rather continued to watch as his former partner rode away, growing smaller by the second.

She wanted to ask if he believed her to be a curse but didn't dare. What if he said yes?

Jed sighed, looked at the ground. There was a defeated slope to his shoulders as he hooked his thumbs into his belt. "I suppose I ought to start shoveling. He might have waited until we got the hole dug, at least."

BY THE TIME they were to bury Zeke, the sun had begun its descent, and the air had cooled somewhat, a breeze stirring up dust but also refreshing Melissa's weary soul as she watched Jed carry the body she had wrapped in a sheet to the hole he'd labored over for so long.

How did he manage? After all he'd done, the man had to be on the verge of collapse. Yet there he was, dragging the body across the ground by the sheet Melissa had tied closed in small, even knots.

She'd heard Jed talking to himself about how to best

move Zeke. Carrying him would mean dropping him into the grave, which seemed disrespectful, but so did dragging him by the feet and sliding him into the hole.

That he cared at all spoke to his character. Imagine, a man like him having character. Wonders would never cease.

Once the body was in the hole, she joined Jed. He looked ten years older than the man she'd met only a week or so earlier, haggard and unshaven and sweat-soaked. He stank horribly and swayed on his feet—slightly, but enough for her to notice the occasional brushing together of their arms.

"I don't know what to say," he muttered, scratching the back of his gritty, sunburned neck. "Zeke had his faults, as all men do, but he was loyal. He had his reasons for being who he was—as all men do. I hope I was a good friend to him and I hope he didn't hurt too much there near the end."

"I believe he was truly sorry in his last moments," she murmured, her hands folded. "And that he could have been a good man if things had turned out differently for him."

Jed said nothing. He merely made the sign of the cross over his chest, took the shovel in his dirty hands and began to fill the hole he'd just dug. If she were not with child, she might have offered to help, but she'd put her body through enough while nursing the dying man.

He would not have accepted the offer, anyway.

Instead, there was the matter of food to consider. Travis

had tended the fire and heated their meals. Someone would have to take up the task in his stead.

She fed the fire with a handful of sticks and looked around for something to heat up. A can of beans would have to do. She opened it, poured it into the only pot the four men had possessed among themselves and set the lid on top.

She then went to the river for water to drink with and filled the bucket that she might wash the dishes before using them. Travis had never been one for cleanliness, though she hadn't dared raise her voice in complaint.

It appeared as though she was the lady of the camp now, and as such things would be done her way.

The sky was dark and spangled with stars by the time Jed finished, thrusting the shovel into the mound of earth once the last bit of dirt had been tossed on top.

"I heated you up some food," she offered, motioning to the pot she'd moved from the fire. "There's fresh water in your canteen, and I shook out your bedroll."

He stopped short, frowning—though whether the frown was for her or for what he'd been through, she couldn't say. It was easier to believe the latter.

"Thank you, ma'am." He had never called her that before.

She'd already eaten, which meant there was little else to do but sit and look at the stars. Not that she would ever complain, as she'd never seen anything so wondrous in all her life. There was nothing like it in Boston, that much was certain.

Jed cleared his throat in the midst of eating, and she turned her face his way. "I hate to interrupt you, since you seem so interested in the sky."

"What is it?" she murmured, unwilling to break the peace of the moment. It had been days and days since she'd enjoyed quiet—she'd known nothing but trains, stage-coaches, and the squawking of men for too long.

"I believe there is something we ought to discuss, now that it's just the two of us."

"Which is?" He was stalling, and she knew it, but she still pitied him for the struggle of the last few days, and this made her hold her tongue more than she would have otherwise.

He finished his plate of beans and rested his elbows on his knees. "The way I see it is this; the whole scheme was a mistake from the beginning."

She sat up, now giving him her full attention. "You don't believe what Travis believed, do you? That I've brought you bad luck?"

He snorted, waving his hands. "No, nothing like that. But I do think it was a mistake to bring you along. I thought it would work, but mayhaps this is the Good Lord's way of telling me I reached a bit too far this time. Takin' a woman and all—I never did anything like that before. And here we are, three men down. I'm not fool enough to ignore such a sign as this."

"What are you driving at? Do you plan on abandoning me now?"

He winced. "I wouldn't have put it that way."

"How would you have put it, then?"

"I would've offered to see you to the next town or village and let you go on your way from there."

She bit her lip, considering this. "No. That won't work."

His eyes opened wide. "You can't mean it."

"Why can't I? You've left me with nothing. I have no money, no tickets, nothing. I would have no way to get to Carson City than by horse—and the notion of riding all that way alone seems the height of foolishness."

His mouth worked for a while without sound—then, "Lemme get this straight. You tried to run away from us before. You kicked me in the—in my private parts," he growled. "You called us everything you could think of and told us your husband would have the law on us in no time. I lost track of the number of times you said you hate me. Is this right? Have I told a lie?"

"You're right," she admitted.

"I just wanted to be sure, because now it sounds like you're telling me you wanna stay with me. Am I imagining this? Because I am tuckered out, so I might be imagining it."

"You are not imagining a thing." She stood with all the dignity she could muster and stared him down. "You kidnapped me. It's too late to leave me on my own—it would be the height of cruelty, and if there's anything I learned about you these last few days, it's that you are not by nature a cruel person."

"You might be wrong about that," he muttered, brows lowered over his narrowed eyes.

"I do not think so. I've seen cruelty up close, and it doesn't appear to be in your nature."

"What are you saying, then?"

She smiled. "I'm saying I'm your responsibility now, and you need to see me safely to Carson City, Nevada. As quickly as possible."

12

I f she didn't beat all, he didn't know what did.

There he was, thinking she'd thank him for letting her go. Any sane woman would have, after the hardship he'd treated her to ever since the night he took her from that coach. Watching a man die from a snakebite, camping in the middle of nothing and nowhere. Water from the river, heat from the cooking fire.

Yes, a reasonable woman would have run and not looked back.

Why in the name of hell could he not have taken a reasonable woman?

There she was, standing there with her head high, like she was the queen. She wore a dress he would've wagered had seen a few years of use, one she had worn and washed out in the river for days on end and hung on her like a rag. Her face was nut brown after days in the sun, her hair around as smooth and shining as a tumbleweed.

He had never seen anything so beautiful—or so infuriating, so impossible to understand.

When he offered no response, for there was truly nothing to be said, she continued. "Now that we're alone, just you and me, I think there are a few things we need to get straight. I've done a lot of thinking these last few days. There was little else to do while nursing... him." Her eyes drifted to the pile of dirt covering what used to be his friend.

She sat down, arranging her skirts around her as carefully as a woman might do at a picnic. He supposed they were sort of picnicking, eating under a starry sky instead of in the sunshine. He'd never had a picnic, so he was only guessing.

"What do you wanna get straight?" He finished eating, put the bowl aside. Beans had never tasted so good, but a starving man had little room to be choosy. "I've been pretty upfront with you all this time."

"But I have not been with you, and now, I feel you ought to know a few things." She grimaced, going quiet for a minute.

He guessed she fought with herself over whether she ought to continue. What could a woman like her have to hide? He wouldn't have guessed she had any secrets.

She looked down at her hands. "You see, it is very important that we get to the Furnish ranch quickly. We've lost time already, too much time. I would have been there by now, had it not been for the stage robbery. Or perhaps not. I've lost track of the days."

"It's been about two weeks," he confirmed.

"I feared as much."

Feared? "What are you so worked up about? You keep talkin' about being in a hurry, but you won't say why."

"That's why I wanted to speak with you now. Just be patient and let me speak."

"I'm a little too tired for patience at the moment, thank you." And filthy, and sore, and more than a little sad.

"Fine, then. I'm on my way to Carson City to marry Mark Furnish. I am not yet Mrs. Furnish. He's waiting for me, so we can marry there."

His jaw fell open. Never would he have expected that.

"So, now you see. He sent for me, paid for my tickets. He'll be waiting, which means he'll be even more likely to send out the law when I don't arrive."

He'd been rendered speechless for the first time in his life. Completely speechless. After what he'd been through not just on that day but the few leading up to it, this was what would break him. He was sure of it.

She took advantage of his stunned silence. "I traveled under his name for the sake of—how can I say it plainly— deference from the menfolk. You must be aware that men treat a woman better when they know she's married. Like a brand has been placed on her rump." She sneered, still looking at her hands.

He'd touched her hands, hadn't he? They were small, warm, the fingertips callused. He'd held them when she whimpered in the tent, the day of the big storm.

"So, I asked Mr. Furnish to purchase the tickets as

though he was doing so for his wife. After all, I was to become his wife upon reaching Carson City." She twisted her fingers together. "Everyone aboard the coach called me Mrs. Furnish, and I never corrected them. Just as I never corrected you. I thought you would be gentler with me, knowing I was the man's wife."

His exhausted brain scrambled to keep up with her. All this time, he'd been hoping for a ransom on a fiancée. Not a wife.

Though he still could not make heads or tails of how this changed things, he could only grasp at the notion that it did change them. Quite a bit.

Jed closed his eyes, counting to five before speaking. If he spoke too soon, he might explode.

"You're telling me you're a bride arranged through mail?" he whispered.

Lord, but his chest was tight. Blood rushed hot and fast in his ears, creating a dull roar. What had it all been for? Why had he risked all of their necks?

She sniffed. "What's so wrong with that?"

"Nothing, nothing." He pressed his lips together, blowing a breath out of his nose. He sounded like a steer on the ranch that slowly faded from view. His dream, disappearing into a mist.

"This doesn't change anything."

"Like hell, it doesn't!" He picked up the tin bowl he'd only just discarded and threw it as hard as he could.

She shrank away from the sound of it clattering against a rock.

"Do you see what you did? You led me out here all this way, let me think you were somebody you weren't! You don't mean a damn thing to the man! And here I was, thinking I could get the money I need!" It came out as a yell, almost a sob, wrenched from the depths of his heart. Frustrated, dismayed, bitter.

"I do mean something to him! He needs a wife, and I'm to be that wife! He's waiting for me, and the longer he waits, the more likely he'll be to give you whatever you want when I arrive!" She stood, facing him in spite of the drawn, frightened look in her eyes. "If you would have let me finish what I had to say before throwing a fit, you would see how this can work out for both of us!"

They glared at each other, both of them breathing heavy. He would gladly have broken her neck just then; his hands twitched as though they longed to do so. He shoved them into his pockets.

"What?" he snarled. "What else is there?"

She pressed one hand to her throat, one to her stomach. Her chest rose and fell rapidly as she breathed in short, shallow bursts. "I think I'm a little more worn out than I thought."

He took her by the arms, stricken with the way she looked and sounded. In all this time, she hadn't shown a bit of weakness or fatigue. "Here. Sit. Drink some water. Breathe slow."

She nodded as she took the canteen from him, drinking deeply of the water within. Damn it, she had overworked herself. He might have slaved away over a grave, but she had been washing the bedding and airing out the tent, fixing the food and seeing to his comfort. And she'd gotten just about as much sleep as he had when Zeke was ill, too.

When she caught her breath, and her face got back some of its color, she whispered, "I thought if you were my escort instead of the man who kidnapped me, Mr. Furnish would be in a more generous mood when we arrived."

He considered this as she rested with her eyes closed. She was willing to pretend he had helped her, rather than tell the truth of who he was? Why would she do that? She didn't owe him anything. Could he trust her?

He'd trusted her up to that point, ever since Zeke was sick. She could have easily taken one of the horses and fled. In his distress over Zeke's condition, he would've let her go. Travis would have, too, seeing as how he thought she was a curse.

Instead, she had not only stayed, but she'd helped him. He never could've done it all on his own.

"How would we work it out?" he asked, already half sold on the idea.

Her eyes fluttered open. "I would tell him I escaped the bandits and you found me, lost and exhausted and afraid. I might have starved to death if it weren't for you, or been picked up by a band of Indians. Something like that. And you saw to my safety and protected me the rest of the way."

It might work. It might certainly work. If she could be convincing, Furnish might be even more likely to hand over a hefty sum for delivering his bride-to-be. A man did not need to go so far out of his way, to protect a strange woman. To save her life, even.

And there was no one to contradict their story.

"I'll need to think this over," he said, putting an abrupt end to the discussion. "It's late, I'm just about falling asleep with my eyes open. I need a bath somethin' terrible. And you need to rest, too. We have a long way to go."

For once, she didn't argue.

He woke well after dawn the next morning, fresh with determination.

As was usually the case, a good night's sleep had helped clear his head. What seemed like a decent idea the night before was now the only course of action they could rightly take. It would be another few days of travel straight through Utah Territory if the weather held, then maybe another week until they crossed Nevada.

If they dawdled any longer, Furnish might wonder what had taken so long. Jed wanted the man in good spirits when they arrived, wanted to be lauded as a hero for having brought Melissa safely to him.

The more heroic he seemed, the more he could collect.

Imagine. Him, a hero.

He sat up in the shadow of the tent and stretched, feeling better than he had in days. Yes, the sight of Zeke's grave was a vise gripping his heart, but he would have to keep moving in spite of the sadness of it. Death came to everyone. He only wished Zeke's had been quicker.

But Melissa had done all she could to make it easier for

him. She'd been an angel to a man who had not deserved her mercy.

The memory of those tender moments made him search the area for her. The tent was silent, there was no cooking fire. Was she still asleep?

He stood outside the flap and cleared his throat. And again. No stirring inside. It would be up to him to get things started that morning, then.

The first trip would be to the river, where he would wash up and fill the canteens. He gathered them, humming to himself a bit; it was easy to be in a lighthearted mood on a beautiful morning, after having gotten enough sleep.

Until the sound of quiet retching swept all pleasant thoughts aside.

He paused, tilting his head in the direction of the noise. It had to be Melissa, unless someone had snuck into their camp with the intention of vomiting.

He found her on the other side of the brush line, on her hands and knees. She let out a strangled gagging noise which turned his stomach before coughing something up, then breathed heavily while waiting for it either to pass or for something else to come up.

She covered up the mess, using her hands to sweep loose soil over it, before going to the water's edge and rinsing her mouth, then splashing her face and the back of her neck with cold water.

She had done this before. There was a skilled nature to her movements. Vomit, cover it up, wash her hands, rinse her mouth. As though this was just another chore she performed every morning.

Every...

"Why are you still lying to me?"

His voice was like a bullet piercing the otherwise peaceful morning air, and Melissa jumped before whirling about. She was pale, as she had been the night before, and now he understood why. He understood it all.

"Why did you lie last night?" He barged through the brush and threw the canteens to the ground. "Why didn't you tell me everything?"

"What are you talking about?" But there was none of the strength or fire in her voice that he'd come to know so well. Because she knew he had her dead to rights this time.

He went to her, stopped just short of taking her arms and shaking her until her head bobbed like a rag doll's. "Why didn't you tell me you were going to have a baby?"

13

S he couldn't answer right away, the surprise of him finding her and accusing her of the truth were too much for words to fight through.

And she had been so careful, getting sick as quietly as she could every morning, fighting through nausea in the back of the wagon as it jolted her from side to side. She was skilled in the art of concealing illness, as there had always been somebody else to take care of. The boys, her mama, her husband.

"Why don't you answer me?" Jed demanded. "Why didn't you tell me of this? Do you know how dangerous it is for a woman to work as hard as you have when she's in this condition? Do you know what might have happened if you fell, or if one of the horses kicked you? You did fall, damn it! Out of the wagon!"

He turned away, running his hands through his hair.

"Damn it and damn you. Why did you lie last night, when you told me it was time to share the truth?"

"I did share the truth!" she gasped, finally finding her voice.

Not that it mattered much. He spun around, his normally handsome face a mask of fury. "You told the part of the truth you thought was worth telling, which isn't the same at all!"

"Are you angry because I didn't tell you about the child, or because I might have been hurt?"

This seemed to knock some of the fire out of him, and when he spoke again, there was no shouting. "Both. I don't know what I would do with a woman bleeding out from a... whatever it's called. But I know it can be nasty, and I know there are times when a woman can die if she doesn't get help. I wouldn't know what to do."

She'd never heard anybody sound so miserable, and to her surprise, she felt sorrier than she had in a long time. "Forgive me," she whispered. "I didn't want anybody to know. Anybody at all."

"I can understand why," he sneered.

"You think I'm one of those women, then?" she challenged. "The type who gets herself in this condition by a man outside of marriage?"

"You already told me you're not married to Mark Furnish, that he bought your tickets and sent 'em to you. What else is there to think?"

He hated her. He had no respect for her—if he'd ever had any at all, but she thought he might have. He'd been kinder to her as of late. Gentler. Likely because of Zeke and their working together. That sort of thing had a way of bringing people together.

Now, there was more contempt in his voice than there had ever been when he'd hurled the name Furnish at her as though it were a curse.

He laughed, throwing his hands into the air. "And that's why you're in such an awful hurry to get there. Gods, Jed, you're so stupid!" Another laugh, full of bitterness. "You want him to think the bastard is his!"

"Do not call my child a bastard," she warned. "I grew up with three of them under my roof, thank you very much, and they were good boys. Sweet boys who had to become young men far sooner than they should have because of how they were born. No fathers to look after them. I had to be their father as best I could until they went out to steal food just, so we might survive."

Instead of warming his heart, this made him even colder. "Then I would think you'd be smart enough not to do that to another child—making them a bastard as your brothers were."

"This child isn't a bastard!"

"If it's not your husband's, it is!"

"*It is my husband's!*" Her announcement echoed across the river, up to their camp, making birds take flight in the nearby trees.

He let out a long breath, as though all the air left his lungs at once. Melissa instantly regretted saying it—the one thing she'd sworn never to tell another living soul.

"Your husband?" he asked, squinting. "You already have a husband?"

She closed her eyes to keep the world from spinning out of control all around her. If she saw it spinning, she would only get sick again. "I have a husband in Boston—at least, I think he's my husband. A man came and spoke the vows and John gave me this." She held up her left hand, where the gold band still sat. "That was a little more than a year ago. We couldn't afford five of us in the house anymore, and there was no room with the boys growing as they were. I married John Carter so I could get out of there. And now I'm going to marry Mark Furnish so I can get away from Boston and never, ever go back."

She waited in silence for something. Some word, some gesture, something. Even if he cursed her, at least that would be saying something. Anything would be better than the stony silence.

When he touched her hand, she flinched.

"Relax," he murmured, and when she opened her eyes, he was leading her to a fallen log a little ways down, near the water.

She sat, and he stood before her with the sun to his back. The glare made it difficult to see his face, to judge what he must think of her.

"He was the one who hurt you." It was not a question, and there was no use in denying it.

"Very much. Nearly every day in one way or another. I lost three teeth in the back of my mouth. There's a scar on the back of my head, under my hair. You asked if I ever saw a dislocated shoulder getting set? I set my own, a month after the wedding."

He turned his face to the side, spitting out a stretch of foul words.

"That's just the big things. There were black eyes, sprains, split lips. And the screaming and the terrible words. Over and over. I had to get away from him. When I wrote to Mark Furnish in answer to his ad, I only wanted a way to get out of Boston. I didn't really intend to marry him. But then..."

"But then you found out about the baby," he finished.

"Yes. I couldn't... I didn't..." She covered her face with her hands, suddenly full to overflowing with shame. Shame for who she was and what she'd done by telling so many lies, shame over someone else knowing all that had been done to her. He probably thought her weak and pitiful, just as John always had.

Gravel shifted under his feet as he drew nearer, but she did not dare uncover her face to look at him. "You don't need to explain any further," he assured her in a quiet voice. "I understand well enough now."

"I... I couldn't... I just..." The tears wouldn't stop, nor would the shoulder-shaking sobs which seemed to come from a place deeper than her heart. From her toes, maybe, all the way up to where they poured from her mouth.

"Breathe." He sat beside her, his warmth and solidness a slight comfort. It was better than nothing.

"I'm sorry," she sobbed, shaking her head at herself and her folly.

"Sorry for what?" His voice reminded her of the way she once spoke to the boys when they were little and hurting over something.

"Lying. Bringing you into this. It's illegal, what I'm going to do."

"If the marriage to your husband in Boston was ever legal, like you said," he reminded her. "But nobody has to know. I won't tell anyone."

"You won't?" She dared raise her head, knowing she must look a fright—eyes red and swollen, face flushed and wet, nose running.

Rather than criticize, he handed her a handkerchief from his back pocket. "I won't. I couldn't send you back to him. And in case you forgot..." He looked around them, as though he had a secret. "I don't care much about abidin' by the law."

The fact that he would joke shocked her out of her misery and pulled a laugh from her.

"Is there anything else I need to know? Anything at all?" Something clouded his eyes, tightened his jaw. "Did he know where you were going?"

She shook her head. "I did everything I could to hide it from him. Do you think I would be here and breathing if he knew?"

"A fair question." He patted her leg—a casual gesture, as one would pat the leg of a friend—then stood. "Wash up, get yourself ready to go. It seems we're in more of a hurry than I thought."

She blinked hard, the last of her tears overflowing and

coursing down her cheeks. "You mean it? You're really going to keep my secret?"

He hooked his thumbs into his belt loops. "Seems to me we both have a secret the other is keeping. That seems pretty much fair. Don't you think?"

It was more than fair. It was a relief greater than anything she'd ever known.

And that was what shot her from the log and into him, her arms flinging themselves around his neck without her willing them to, her head against his shoulder before she could stop herself.

"Thank you, thank you," she murmured against the rough work shirt, the smell of leather and horse and man mingling together like a strange cologne she was becoming quite fond of.

He hesitated before winding his arms around her waist. Slowly, as though she might burn at the touch. "You're safe now. You don't need to worry about a thing."

To her surprise, she believed him.

14

"Take a look down there." Jed pointed over the edge of the ridge they'd just driven up to. Flat, grassy land stretched out as far as the eye could see to the north, south, and west. A silver ribbon of river cut through to the north, where hundreds of head of cattle were drinking their fill and grazing on the thick, emerald grass while a dozen cowboys rode up and down the line to keep the stock together.

Melissa stood, shielding her eyes from the sun. She'd lost the bonnet somewhere in Utah, when a stiff wind blew it off her head, the one and only time she'd worn it untied. Since then, the sun had turned her hair from gold to nearly white.

With the blue sky framing her, her slim body clothed in his extra shirt and trousers—there was no wearing that dress of hers, not if she intended to still have a dress to wear once they reached their destination—she made a striking sight. It was rare that he allowed himself the luxury of staring at her, but he couldn't help himself just then.

There were times when her beauty just about knocked him over, even when she wore men's clothes several sizes too big.

"That's ranchland?" she asked, watching the cattle and the cowboys with rapt attention, unaware of the way he admired her.

"Yep, that's it. That's what you'll be lookin' at a lot of once we reach Furnish Ranch. Thousands and thousands of acres." He couldn't help but note the way his chest tightened at the thought of Mark Furnish and his great big ranch. All the money he had.

And soon, a wife. Melissa.

In a little more than a week, more than likely.

They had crossed into Nevada the day before by his estimation. It would be maybe a week to cross the state if the weather held.

While he knew how important it was for her to reach Carson City in quick fashion, he couldn't help but wish for a string of stormy days.

That was selfish, and one thing he'd always prided himself on was being unselfish.

But then, he'd never known her. He'd never known what it meant to want a woman all to himself.

She sat back down, beside him, and he steered the team right, so they might skirt the edge of the ridge and continue northwest. Soon they would simply drive west, all the way out until they reached the state capital.

"It's hard living, ranch life," Melissa informed him.

She did not yet know he had no need for such information, that he'd seen a rancher's life close-up and for many years.

"Is it, now?"

She nodded. "The letter Mr. Furnish wrote to me described it in detail. He didn't make it seem... desirable."

A damned fool, he was. Any other woman than Melissa —one not so desperate to escape her pitiful life—might have read what the idiot wrote and decided against making the long journey.

"He only wanted to be sure I knew what I was getting into," she continued, unaware of the battle he fought with himself every time she brought up the man's name. "He's a very honest man."

Honest. So unlike himself.

Jed had no reason to loathe Furnish, and yet he did. More and more with each passing day, in fact. Each time she smiled or laughed, each time she revealed a bit of herself to him.

Like when he'd found out she taught herself to read.

He'd carry the memory of her flushed cheeks forever, deep in the darkest corner of his heart, and look back on it fondly whenever he needed to smile. She'd been proud of herself, and a little embarrassed. He would've bet both horses and the wagon they were hitched to that she'd never had a reason to be proud of herself before then.

"My—I mean, John—used to bring newspapers into the house," she explained. Jed noticed she corrected herself whenever she was about to call him her husband. "And there were mail-order catalogs, too. When I'd see a picture of something I knew the name of, I would learn the word underneath it. I started learning other words, then before long, I could read sentences once I understood the sounds the letters made. I recognized the words as I was sounding them out by their letters…" She'd let out a little laugh. "You see how it went. It took months, but I got the hang of it."

"What about writing?" he'd asked. She must have written to Furnish, and she'd read his letter in reply. Newsprint and hand-written letters were very different.

Her blush had deepened to one of shame. "When John would go out to work, I would steal into his study and read the letters he received in the post. I knew our name and address, so I knew those letters and words on the envelopes, and I pieced the rest of it together myself. It was like working out a puzzle."

When he'd gaped at her in open-mouthed awe, she'd shrugged. "It gave me something to do. At least I learned something during that year. I can take that away from it."

Whoever this Furnish character was, he'd better deserve a wife like her. Jed had never known anyone with that sort of determination, male or female. And when he considered the sort of household she'd lived in, too…

She got herself out of there the only way she could. By teaching herself to read and write so one day, she could write to a man clear across the country.

Funny, but he'd never considered how hard it was to be a woman. From what he gathered of Melissa's stories, her mother got around quite a bit—or, the men got around to her. That was where the three fatherless boys came from, boys whose names Melissa never mentioned. Maybe it was hard for her to do it. Maybe she wanted to forget them.

But the woman hadn't started off that way. She only started entertaining men when her husband died and left her penniless. He wondered if it was an easy way to earn a meager living, and the only way she could think to keep body and soul together.

In that way, he wasn't that different from her. Nobody grew up wanting to be a bandit, either.

He wondered if Melissa knew how she made him think, how she forced him to question so many things about himself. If she even cared.

Why would she?

She sat there, looking around, leaning her elbows on her spread thighs. He couldn't help but laugh at her change in posture.

"What's so funny?"

That was a tough question to answer, especially when she asked it with suspicion in her voice. Over their weeks together, he'd learned to tread lightly when she took that tone.

"You look mighty comfortable, is all. The trousers suit you."

She looked down, finally aware of the way she'd been sitting, and laughed at herself. "I look like a real lady, don't I? Next thing you know, I'll be spitting tobacco juice."

"Never took up the habit, myself, or I'd share some

tobacco with you just to see you try it."

They shared a smile with too much warmth in it for Jed's comfort. He liked her too damn much. She made him feel lighter than he ever had, even when he was a boy and he had no understanding of life.

"I imagine riding would be easier wearing these," she observed, stretching her legs, spreading them wider.

He wished she'd stop. While there wasn't a hint of awareness in her movements, the animal side of his nature stirred in his loins.

It seemed that animal never strayed far from the surface of his thoughts anymore, always ready to pounce on the slightest action. When she licked her lips to catch a crumb before it fell, or ran her hand over the long, slim column of her neck.

Innocent actions, the simplest things, yet enough to make him grit his teeth and clench his fists and think about awful, bloody, terrible things to push back the animal desire she unleashed.

He wanted to hurry and get her to Carson City before he ran out of willpower and awful images to call into his mind.

He wanted to take his time and come up with reasons to lengthen the trip, that he might spend more time with her. For how could he go back to being alone after her?

They rode half the day this way, in companionable silence. He allowed her to take the reins from time to time, since she insisted, and his arms did grow tired after so many days.

He studied the way she drove the team, her back straight as an arrow, shoulders squared. She took it very seriously, as she took everything she was just learning to do. Like reading and writing, for instance. The woman was determined.

Yes, she'd make a good rancher's wife.

"You're gonna fit right in on a ranch," he observed, leaning against the wooden planks at his back, tipping the brim of his hat over his eyes to rest a bit.

"Do you really think so?"

"Yup, I do."

"Why do you think so?"

She was like a child sometimes, always pressing for more, always asking questions. This brought back memories of a child he used to know, one who followed him wherever he went and asked questions about everything he did.

"Because you're determined. It takes a great deal of determination to help a man run a ranch. You have energy and a keen mind. You're bossy as hell when you have a mind to be. And you don't take guff easily. These are all things he'll need from you."

"I would want my husband to be a success in anything he does," she announced.

He caught a glimpse of the firm set of her jaw from the corner of his eye. Like she was willing it so.

A man would have to be the world's biggest fool to fail with her at his side.

15

Jed grimaced as he climbed down from the wagon.

"What are you so grumpy about?" Melissa asked. "I told you, everything will be all right. Either we get what we need, or we starve." And she was endlessly hungry as of late. While mornings were still unpleasant, once the nausea passed, she almost always wanted something to eat.

In fact, she'd been loosening her stays as of late. Trousers or no trousers, there was no avoiding undergarments, and she had simply not been able to lace as tight as she once had. It was too early for her to start taking the pains all women did to conceal their growing bellies, which meant she was simply putting on weight.

Jed didn't seem to care either way, and his shirt was large enough that she need not feel shame at her growing figure beneath its many folds. She'd taken to wearing the corset simply for the sake of holding things in place.

It was an excuse to be comfortable for once, anyhow.

Thanks to her appetite, they were running dangerously low on just about every supply they had. Travis was the last one to head out for goods, back when Zeke was ill. It seemed a lifetime had passed since then.

She knew Jed would rather not make the stop in town, even if it was little more than a village and even if nobody there could have the slightest chance of knowing them.

"You swear you won't go anywhere without me?" He tilted back his hat, fixing her with a doubtful stare.

"Jed, I'm disappointed in you. Very disappointed."

"That ain't an answer."

"Yes, I swear," she hissed. "There. Are you happy? I swear I won't go anyplace. I'm just going to sit here and wait."

For if she went inside alone, she might tell somebody who she was and who he was. If they went in together and somebody came riding through, later on, asking about a man and a woman seen traveling together, that could be a problem as well.

He'd already worried about this aloud as he shaved in the little looking glass he carried with him. She wondered if he knew just how much he muttered to himself when he was in a mood.

"I guess there's no way of gettin' out of this," he grumbled.

"There isn't. And I'm hungry. Could you please go in and get us some food?"

"Yes, ma'am," he muttered, shaking his head as he

stepped up onto the boardwalk which ran the length of the street. "She's hungry. What a surprise."

She held her tongue only because they were in public and it wouldn't do to have a fight. What mattered most was getting out of there without anybody noticing them.

He walked into the general store, beneath the large-lettered sign advertising its wide range of goods, and she bit her lip as blood rushed to her cheeks. He was a sight to behold, both when he was walking toward her and when he was walking away.

It was all the riding, she decided. His legs and rear were firm, tight, his shoulders strong, his back lean and muscular and enough to make her wonder what it would feel like under her hands, with no fabric to get in the way of his warmth, of the muscles moving under his skin.

She didn't know until pain sprang from her palms that she'd dug her nails into them, and her heart raced beyond all measure.

What was the matter with her? She'd gone mad. That had to be it. And every man, woman, and child who passed the wagon more than likely knew what was going on in her deranged mind just by the flush of her cheeks and the way she stared at the spot where Jed had just stood.

Was it right for a woman to think of a man this way? Normal?

It was certainly sinful, of that she had no doubt. For how could the rush of warmth that coursed throughout her body be anything but?

She'd known of the needs of men for longer than she

cared to remember, the sounds from Mama's bedroom enough to teach her from a young age. And that was before the men started looking at her the way they did, once she grew up some.

That was when her mother had sat her down and given her the facts, plainly and sometimes painfully frank. Men wanted certain things, and it was up to a woman to lie back and let them take what they wanted.

John had spoken of his needs, too, and of the rights of a husband to satisfy those needs—not to mention the duties of a wife to do the satisfying.

No one had ever told her a woman might have needs. John had certainly never inspired anything more than discomfort and displeasure as he sweat like a pig on top of her.

Only Jed had ever made her flush with what she guessed was desire. He made the back of her neck tingle when he looked her in the eye, when his gaze sometimes drifted down to her lips.

And her throat tightened whenever he rode the horses, warming them up one at a time before hitching them for a long day's ride. His capable body, moving up and down in the saddle, and the way he swung his leg over the animal's back as he mounted and dismounted. She could watch that all day.

Was it natural for a woman to sigh without meaning to as she watched a man mount a horse?

She hoped so, for if it wasn't, there was something wrong with her.

If only she had a woman to discuss such things with.

"Well, what do we have here?"

She'd been too busy wrapping herself in warm, delicious memories to notice the approach of a pair of men. One of them leaned against the wagon while the other climbed up beside her before she could stop him.

If it were John, or this was Boston, she would have frozen stiff. Like a rabbit when it knew it was cornered. She would have cowered away from the man. She might have begged him to leave her alone if she found her voice at all.

This was not Boston, and the whiskey-soaked man beside her was not John.

"Get away!" she grunted, shoving her body into his with all her might.

He let out a cry of surprise as he tumbled from the wagon, the horses neighing and pawing the ground over this new threat.

He stumbled to his feet, swaying and slurring filthy swear words, and for the first time since the night her coach had been overtaken, Melissa tasted true fear. For the look in his half-open eyes was exactly the look John Carter used to have before he attacked.

And for the first time in her life, she wished she had a pistol handy.

"What do you think you're doin'?" A second later, Jed burst into the scene, running full-force at her would-be attacker and knocking him to the ground for a second time. He hauled the man halfway up by the collar of his stained, dust-covered shirt and landed a solid blow to his mouth. Blood bloomed on his broken lips as if by magic.

"Jed, don't!" Melissa implored, her eyes darting back and forth as witnesses began to gather in store windows, along the boardwalk.

"He-he didn't mean no harm, mister." The man's friend, clearly in possession of greater sense, put himself between Jed and the man who now bled on the ground, groaning and stunned.

"Jed," Melissa hissed, still keenly aware of their audience. "Let's go. We have to go, now."

There was fire in his eyes when he glanced up at her. "You all right?" He grunted, his chest heaving with each ragged breath.

Dear Lord, he set her blood on fire when he looked like that. Like he would tear the head from the shoulders of any man who dared touch her.

She could only nod. Words failed her.

He loaded the supplies into the wagon, dropped as they'd been when he saw what was taking place in his absence, and she steered the team away from the store and indeed the town the moment he was beside her on the bench.

Only when they were well outside the town, and he pried the reins from her clenched fists did she dare breathe easier.

They rode in silence until night fell and it was time to make camp, and even then, the conversation they held was stilted, broken. Nothing like the usual chatter they fell into.

And she missed that. She hadn't known until just then how she'd come to rely on their talks, the brief stretches of time that was theirs alone. Disappointment soured the inside of her mouth.

She dared ask only one question before ducking into the tent as she always did. "Do you blame me for what happened today? For attracting those men?"

He looked at her, really looked at her for the first time since they rode away from that little no-name place. "Why would I ever blame you for what they did? You had nothin' to do with it. And from what I saw, you made sure he knew you weren't having any of it."

The note of pride in his voice carried her into the tent on wings, and later on, she fell asleep with a smile... and the memory of his flaming eyes, his heaving chest, and how much she'd wished to fall into his arms.

16

He waited until she doused the lantern inside the tent before letting out a long, slow breath and unclenching his fists. His fingers were stiff from being curled so tight for so long.

And the knuckles of his right hand were sore after smashing against that bastard's mouth, back in town. He wished he could've done more. He wished he could've killed the drunken, pitiful wreck of a man who dared to even speak to her.

He might have come closer to doing it if she hadn't stopped him. She was right, of course, she was. The last thing they needed was to attract attention, and attention had found them. The only thing that could've made it worse would be murdering a man in cold blood, out in the open with dozens of people watching.

To think, he'd been nervous about bringing her into the store.

It wasn't the stranger he'd hit. He might have been holding onto the collar of a man who'd been foolish enough to stagger out of a saloon and into a wagon which didn't belong to him, but it was Melissa's husband he saw when he struck.

He didn't even know what the man looked like, but he'd been thinking of him when he swung his fist. Every time he'd hurt her. The injuries she had described and so many others probably too shameful to mention.

Yes. He would've killed the man had she not stopped him in time.

And he had no right to feel that way. He had no right to want to defend her.

To hold her tight and shield her from the world.

To take her into his bed, or bedroll, as the case may be. To make her his under the stars.

He squeezed his eyes shut, willing the images away. They wouldn't fade. They came back stronger, more vivid.

This was what love must be like.

He'd never known it until then—and a good thing, or it might have killed him a long time before. How did men walk through life with their hearts in their throats and an ache in their pants every time they thought about their woman?

But she wasn't his woman. She wasn't, and she never would be. He had killed any chance of that happening when he killed the driver of the stage and taken her as his captive.

No. Sooner.

Many years ago.

The sound of screaming. His mother's.

His own.

He was not a good man, and certainly not worthy of a woman like the one sleeping in the tent.

"WE OUGHT to reach the city tomorrow, isn't that right?" Melissa counted the days on her fingers. "It's been eight days now since we crossed into Nevada."

"That's right." Jed's heart was heavy as he pulled the wagon up to the edge of a ridge, as it had been not long after they'd crossed the border.

That day, he'd pointed out a working ranch to her, knowing there was still a week between then and this moment. He'd kept her ignorant as to how close they'd been drawing to Carson City all day, each mile they rolled took them one mile closer to saying goodbye.

It was best for her, and for the child. This was the only thought which kept him moving. It was for the best that he sacrifice his feelings for her.

It was all he could do for her, making sure she started a new life with a better man than her first husband—a better man than himself, more likely than not.

He set the brake, pointing over the ridge to the valley below. "You know what that is?" he asked with a bucketful of false cheer.

Her eyes went round. "We're here? That's it?"

"That's it." It shone like a jewel. That was the only way he could think to describe it. The capitol dome stood out over all others, a flag waving proudly from above it. In spite of the smoke from approaching freight trains which were like a dark cloud over the city, the tree-lined streets seemed downright welcoming from afar.

Melissa let out a soft laugh. "After all this time, it seemed like we would never get here. But here we are. It's real."

"And it's your new home," he reminded her—and himself. She belonged there. She would be safe there, more comfortable than he could ever make her.

"My new home," she whispered, as though she was trying out the words for size, seeing if they fit in her mouth. "I suppose we ought to get going, then..."

"I suppose."

Neither of them moved.

"He might be waiting for me," she added.

"Might be? He'd be the world's biggest fool if he wasn't."

She smiled, looked down at her folded hands. "You're just saying that."

"I have no reason to just say that. He'll be waiting at the ranch for word of you. It would be merciful for us to get down there and find a way to get word to him, I reckon."

"It would."

So why did she sound hesitant? He didn't dare pretend it was for him. He was still her kidnapper. He'd kept her away from her new husband for two precious weeks, weeks when her baby was growing and making it less likely for Mark Furnish to believe he was the father.

"Do you think we ought to wait until morning?" he asked, keeping his gaze trained on the horizon for fear that if he looked at her, his entire heart would be written on his face and she'd see him for who he was. A lovesick fool.

She remained quiet. What was she thinking? Likely she wanted to hurry and get to her new husband and was only trying to spare his feelings.

Could he blame her? Mark Furnish meant everything. The sort of life she could've only dreamed of up until then. Not to mention the hope of security, a little kindness from the man whose name she would take.

She needed the marriage. So did her child.

"If you think we ought to go, we can go," he offered. "Maybe somebody can ride out to his ranch and let him know you arrived safely. He can come to town and get you. Maybe treat you to a late supper, get you a room at the hotel. Or take you..."

"Home," she murmured. "He could take me home."

"That's right."

All he heard for a while was the sound of her breathing.

"You know you don't need to feel any sort of... I don't know, loyalty to me or anything like that," he muttered, pulling the brim of his hat lower. "My feelings won't be sore if you hurry off to your new life. You done waited long enough thanks to me—you would've been here weeks ago."

"I know that."

"So? What do you think?" He dared take a look at her out of the corner of his eye. Hoping. Hardly daring to move.

"I think I might be afraid."

"Afraid?" This was enough to turn him toward her. "Afraid of what?"

"Of running from one thing and straight into the same thing, just someplace else."

"You don't know that. You have to take a chance, is all."

"But what if..." She swallowed, pressed her lips tightly together. Lips he longed to kiss. "What if..."

"If it makes you feel better, I'll stay in town for a little while. You could always come and find me if you need to— if he turns out to be the same type of man as before."

"You would do that?" She gaped at him, open-mouthed. "Truly? It might be dangerous for you."

"It might be, but no one knows who I am, or how we came about being together this way."

It was a damned fool thing to do, and that was a fact. He ought to make tracks out of Carson City the minute the money was in his hand. Instead, he'd just offered to put the noose around his own neck. And all for her.

And she would never understand why he did it, because he could sure as hell never tell her.

That would mean admitting he loved her.

He managed to maintain a bit of a smile, something he hoped encouraged her. "All right? I'll hang around, and I'm sure you could get your hands on a way to get back to me if you needed to. Make an excuse to go to town. You'll need clothes, you'll need personal things."

"That's true." She chewed her lip, staring into the distance over his shoulder. The light of the setting sun reflected in her eyes, shone in the hair which drifted around her face where it came loose from its braid.

He took stock of every inch of her at that moment, letting her soak into his brain and his heart that he might never let her go.

"All right," she agreed. "I suppose we'll set up here for the night and we'll move on in the morning."

They did not meet each other's eyes as they set up. He knew it would be a mistake to look at her for too long.

17

"I never thought I would come to enjoy cooking over a campfire—or that I would be good at it." She cast a look Jed's way. "Keep your opinions to yourself, if you don't mind."

He chuckled, shook his head. "No, no. I was gonna agree with you. It's been a real treat, eating decent food. I never could make a decent cornbread. Always came out hard as a rock."

"You left it on the fire too long, I would wager—or you needed to move it further from the center." She smeared a bit of pork fat onto a slab and ate it with great relish.

"I'll keep that in mind the next time I get a hankering for it."

What had just struck her as the most delicious thing she'd wrapped her lips around in recent memory went as dry and tasteless as sawdust. She struggled to swallow it down.

It was a natural thing to say. She would be leaving him the next day. He would have to fend for himself after then.

Natural or not, Jed's words hung over her heart like a black storm cloud. A heavy as the iron skillet in which she'd baked the bread.

She'd been in such a haste to get away from him.

Now?

There was no telling how she felt. It was all such a mixed-up mess. She might easily have continued on into the city. In fact, it would have looked normal for her to be in a hurry to get there.

She'd been in a hurry before, thanks to the baby. She should've hurried if for that reason alone, to get the bedding over with and start the process of making Mark Furnish believe he was the father.

Yet she'd agreed to spend one last, uncomfortable night outdoors. She'd all but jumped at the chance, had fought against the impulse to agree too quickly for fear of making her eagerness obvious.

He ate in silence except for the sound of chewing. There was no telling how he felt about anything, ever. He'd rather put on a mask and hide himself than show a hint of real, human feeling—outside of rage, of course, considering the way he'd beaten that man outside of the general store.

Maybe it was for the best that there'd never be anything between them, since she didn't know how she'd live with a man who kept everything bottled up inside.

She'd already lived with one who flared into temper at

the slightest inconvenience, after all. Was there a man alive who shared himself naturally, normally, who didn't run only hot or cold?

"You know what we're going to say tomorrow?" she asked, if only for a reason to speak. If he expected her to spend the entire night in silence—their last night together —he had something else coming.

"Of course."

A man of few words, as always, when all she wanted was to hear more from him. To carry something with her once they parted ways. What else would she have to hold in her heart? To pore over every night before falling asleep?

"What are you going to do with the money?"

His brows lifted. "The money from Mr. Furnish?"

"No. The money from the bank you're going to rob when we arrive in the city."

His laughter warmed her, made the back of her neck tingle pleasurably. "A silly question, I admit." He settled back, folding his arms over his chest, pursing his lips. "I would purchase a little parcel for myself."

"Land?"

"Yes, land." He cut his eyes to her. "I'm not as quick with comebacks as you are, or else I would've given you a taste of your own medicine."

She giggled. It was so nice to be with him when he was in a pleasant mood. Would she ever have imagined enjoying the company of a man prior to meeting him?

"A parcel of land, then," she prompted.

"Yeah. Just something small. But something of my own. What I always wanted."

She cast her memory back to past conversations. "You know a lot about ranching. Is that what you want to do?"

He nodded. "I was supposed to have a set-up of my own one day—my father's, when he passed it down. Or I would have, as the oldest son."

She clenched her fists out of sight, hidden in her skirts. "What happened?"

He chuckled without humor. "That's not the sort of thing a man can tell over the course of a single supper."

"Does it look like I have anywhere else to go?" *Please, please, please tell me. I want so much to know you. I want so much to feel close to you.*

He stretched out his legs, crossing them at the ankle. His chest rose and fell when he took a deep breath. "My father disowned me years ago. Never saw him or my Ma again after that."

"Oh." What else was there to say? She imagined he'd stolen from them or done something foolish which had brought harm to the cattle. Leaving a fence open, some lazy thing a young man would do.

His eyes shifted, moved over her face. "Don't you wanna know why?"

"It's none of my business."

"You don't have the slightest bit of curiosity, then?"

"No."

"I thought you always tried to be honest."

She let out a heavy sigh. "It seems you want to tell me, but you want me to push you into it. If it makes you feel better, fine. I want you to tell me why your father disowned you."

His mouth quirked up in a wry smile. "You've got my number, sure as shootin'. Can't put anything past you. But I ain't never told anybody before, is all. Not even Zeke, and he was the closest thing I had to a brother in all these years."

"Did your brother push you away, then, too?" she asked, sympathy building. She knew then that she'd likely fallen in love with the rascal, as all she felt was sorry for him. No blame for whatever it was he'd done to earn his place outside the family. She merely wanted to know what they'd felt was too great to forgive.

His brow creased, his mouth drawing into a thin line. "Nope. I killed him."

She felt as though she'd just jumped into a body of near-frozen water, as though the very blood in her veins had gone solid. "You..."

"Killed him. Yep. I did." He sounded so casual, as though they were discussing the cost of feed or the next day's weather. Not as though they discussed the end of his brother's life, certainly.

"You can't mean it. It must have been—"

"What makes you think I don't mean it, huh?" He was on his feet so suddenly, she jumped back. Away from him.

He would not let her get away that easily. He leaned over her, blocking out the view of the campfire and everything else. All she could see was him, all there was in the world was him.

She was through being cornered.

"Get away from me." She said it with teeth clenched, barely moving her lips. "I mean it. Get. Back. You don't frighten me, so stop trying to."

He blinked like he might be unsure whether she meant it, but he did back away. "There's something I need you to know, something about me that will never change. I need you to remember this when I leave you with your fiancé tomorrow."

"What?" she whispered.

"I am not a good man. I don't know when you got the notion in your head that I am—when Zeke was so sick, or when you had your accident, maybe? But that is not who I am. Do not make the mistake of thinking so. Do you understand?"

She nodded. It was all she could do. Oh, he was so angry, so hateful.

Toward her? There was no telling. Weeks earlier, she might have believed herself to be the one he lashed out at.

Now?

"What did you do, then?" she challenged. "Since you are such a terrible person, you must be proud of what you did. Or at least proud of the telling of it. The shock it stirs in those who listen."

His scowl slipped. "Do not test me. When will you ever tire of testing me?"

Her answer was simple, delivered in a low voice which

belied the steel behind it. "When you tire of huffing and stomping your feet to prove what an evil man you are. I have seen callousness, Jed. I've seen heartless, cold, unfeeling men who had nothing but hate in their hearts. You are not one of those men."

"There are all kinds of bad men in the world, Melissa." He sat again, on a rock closer to her than he'd been before. "Even if they don't mean to do bad, they end up doing bad anyway. It's just their way. How they were born, I reckon."

"And you think you're one of them."

"I don't have to think. I know." He removed his hat, something she rarely saw him do, and turned it in his hands. "Even when I try to do right, something always happens to ruin everything."

"When you told me to leave you, so that I might go on by myself?"

He snickered, eyes still on the sweat-stained, battered hat. "Yeah. Sort of like that."

"Your thoughts were in the right place. You meant well."

"Don't you see? That doesn't matter worth a damn when things still go to hell. What difference does it make that I wanted to do the right thing when I didn't end up doing it?"

There was no answer to this question, for how many times had Melissa tried to do what was right? As a girl, she'd sacrificed her share of the meager bits of food she'd scavenged for the sake of her brothers, that they might eat more. She'd told them time and again how wrong it was to steal, how wicked to lie.

And yet she'd stolen Mark Furnish's money when she'd first asked him to send passage to Carson City, as there had been no intention of marrying him then. Her brothers had become thieves the moment they were old enough to pick pockets.

Both acts were done in hopes of survival, but was that enough to wipe a sin clean from a person's soul?

Jed knew nothing of her silent questions, as he was lost in tormented thoughts. They played upon the face she knew so well, muscles twitching, eyes which held the power to set her soul aflame narrowing and darkening with each memory.

He did not wish to be comforted.

There were ways to comfort a person without doing it outright. Memories of the night she'd bared her soul tugged at her, a reminder of the great weight she'd released after confessing her secrets.

After drawing a deep breath and sending up a silent prayer, she asked, "How did your brother die?"

He shot her a withering look. "Did I hear that right?"

"You can tell me. We'll never see each other again after tomorrow." The words all but stuck in her throat, yet she managed to pretend as though it did not matter.

His eyes were heavy as he studied her. Was he asking himself whether this was a wise idea? Or what her motives might be? Whether she was trustworthy? He had to know by then the answer to that, after all they'd been through.

When his shoulders relaxed, she knew he'd come to a

decision, and braced herself for what she was about to hear.

The brim of his hat curled in tightened fingers, he began, "I was sixteen years old. This was before the war started, but not much before. We were just finishing a branding—you've never seen one, but you will. Or you'll at least see the men coming back from it and wonder how they stay on their feet. Days of work, wrangling and roping. And there were so many calves that spring."

She didn't want to think of what she'd see when he was no longer a part of her life.

He sighed. "Jasper only wanted to prove himself. It was the first thing he thought of in the morning and the last thing on his mind when he fell asleep. How he could prove, he was a man. Ten years old that spring, and he begged Pa from sunup to sundown in the days before we got the branding crew together to let him tag along. I finally told Pa I didn't mind—it was the first year I'd be heading things up, and I guess I was feeling generous, you know."

She nodded.

"But I told him not to get in the way," Jed muttered. "I warned him; step out of line just once, get in the way of what a man was fixin' to do just one time, and that would be it. I'd spank his behind shiny and send him to the house in front of all the men, just to make sure he was good and ashamed."

"And did you have to?" she asked, remembering the times she'd threatened her brothers with similar punishment for their mischief.

He shook his head. "Didn't get the chance, you see. He behaved himself those first two days. He just wanted to watch, to be part of it. To hear the men talking and joking and feel like he was one of us. And I did think I was a man, sure enough. Full of myself, struttin' about like I owned the place. I would one day, you see, so I figured I might as well get myself used to it. Sixteen years old and not the first idea about life, but I thought I knew it all. Right up to the minute I fell from my saddle in the middle of roping a calf."

His voice faded to silence and remained that way for a long, weighty minute.

Melissa's teeth were on edge, her breath barely coming at all as she waited. Did she want to hear? It was too late to ask him to stop—he was there, in that day, on that horse. Falling from its back.

"A stupid thing," he continued with a catch in his voice. "I was showin' off, proud that I had roped thirty already that day when some of the men had to stop at twenty before turning the job over to somebody else. I was tired, really, and my reflexes were slow. When the calf doubled back, trying to get away, my horse reared rather than trample it. And I fell."

"For two days, Jasper kept to himself. For two days, he stood by and watched. Watched me fall down in the muck, watched me get my shirt near torn off. The same with the other men, some of them gettin' hurt for real. It can be dangerous work. But he stayed where I told him to stay and didn't get in the way."

He hung his head. "Until I fell, and he ran for me."

Melissa's eyes filled with tears.

"We're talkin' about a two-hundred-plus-pound calf who was already frightened half out of his wits. When he saw Jasper running for me, right through the path he was already running, he just kept going. Right over my baby brother."

There was no stopping herself from imagining one of the boys in that position, trampled to death in front of her.

"I'll never forget the screams. Not Jasper's—he didn't have time to scream. If there's a God up there in Heaven, he never knew what hit him. It was the kick to the head that did it. I was the one who screamed. Me and the other men, but me most of all. At least Pa wasn't there to see it, nor Ma. I don't think she would have survived hearing her favorite son's head kicked open."

"My Lord." Melissa turned her face away, struggling to contain the sobs which tore at her.

"He was the favorite. The baby. Ma couldn't have any more after the two of us—she lost three in the six years between us, you see, and the doc advised her not to put herself through it again. Jasper was sort of a miracle, I guess you could say. Everybody's pet. And I got him killed. And I had to carry his body back to the house and look into her eyes and my father's eyes and tell them what happened. Pa ordered me off the land that very day."

"He didn't!"

"He did." Jed stared at his Stetson, turning it over and over. "I know if he had the time to think it over instead of just ordering me that way, he wouldn't have done it. He wasn't the sort who took revenge or anything like that, but he changed that day. He told me never to come back, that I was disowned because I let my brother die when I was supposed to protect him. And Ma was half out of her mind, she didn't know what was what. So there was no one to stand up for me. I had to go."

"You never went back?"

"I never dared. Besides, the war came the next year, and I signed up. I wrote home once, two years in, just to tell my ma that I was fightin' and still loved her and was sorry for what I did. I got a letter back from the old foreman, telling me they were both dead and the ranch was getting sold off in pieces. Never did tell me how they died, but I guess it doesn't matter. Dead is dead."

Tears coursed down Melissa's cheeks when she went to him, kneeling at his feet. "You didn't kill Jasper. It wasn't your fault."

He did not look at her. "It was."

"It wasn't!"

"You weren't there." His head snapped around, eyes burning—or was it the reflection of the fire behind her in his eyes. "You don't know. Argue anything you like until your face goes blue, but do not argue that because you were not there to see."

"I don't have to see to know," she insisted. When he turned away once again, she reached for his chin, turning him back to her. "You weren't responsible. It was an accident. Your father was hurting terribly that day, he said things he likely didn't mean." He tried to yank himself out of her grasp, but she held firm.

"Listen to me." She raised herself on her knees until they were face-to-face. "You were not at fault. It wasn't you. You would never have hurt your brother. He ran to help you because he loved you, but you did not make him do it. He was a boy, acting before he thought. You couldn't have known he would."

"I should have."

Her hands cupped his face. "You couldn't have. And the way he looked up to you? The way he ran to help when he thought you might be hurt? I'd bet he would hate to see you tear yourself up over this as you have."

His eyes shone with unshed tears as he took her face the way she held his. When he drew her to him, his mouth seeking hers, she did not resist.

Heat she had never known stirred to life deep inside her core, making her nerves sing and dance, sending goose-flesh in ripples up and down her arms. Jed's hands moved from her face to her lower back, pulling her closer, his powerful arms wrapping her up until there was nothing to do but melt against him. It would be pointless to fight.

Especially since she did not wish to.

Instead, she ran her hands through his thick hair, indulging herself in its softness before sliding them down to his shoulders. Muscles moved beneath shirt and skin, shifting and flexing and turning her fingers into claws as she gripped him.

It was just as she had imagined, only more so. She had

never guessed at the sudden flaring of heat all through her body, the desire to tear at his clothes and feel his hands on her bare skin, all over her. To look into his eyes and know he wanted the same things.

And all the while he kissed her, tongue probing and caressing, drawing a moan from the back of her throat. She'd never moaned while being kissed before.

Compared to this, she'd never been kissed.

There was nothing in the world she wanted more than to give herself to him, to offer what comfort she could, to love him just once before leaving him forever. Would that they could lie together in front of the fire until the sun rose, touching and kissing and creating something she would remember forever.

Instead, the instant Jed's arms tightened with new need, need which seemed to echo the need in her, he pulled his mouth from hers and turned his face away.

"Forgive me," he growled, his breathing harsh.

She touched her forehead to his shoulder, closing her eyes, her breathing matching his. It was not meant to be, and they both knew it.

"There is nothing to forgive," she managed to whisper as she struggled to regain her self-control.

18

There were no words between them as he hitched the team up that morning. It was a bright, clear day, and all of Carson City stretched out before them when they reached the crest of the rise on which they'd spent the night.

One of the longest, most troubled nights of Jed's life.

He watched Melissa from the corner of his eye as she took in the city. "I feel like God, watching from on high," she murmured, a half-smile pulling up the corners of her mouth.

Indeed, there was a feeling of looking down on the city as it went about its morning—already busy for so early in the day, he noted. A freight train pulled into the yard near the northeast corner, black smoke belching from its stack. Several buggies ran up and down what appeared to be the main street, where the state's Capitol building stood head and shoulders over the rest. On what looked like farms at the city's far corners were workers already in the fields.

"I suppose we ought to get down there," he observed, watching the activity. From so high up, the city was quiet, unassuming. That would change once they were in the thick of it, he knew. Especially once word spread that the future wife of Mr. Mark Furnish was in town.

"I suppose so," Melissa whispered.

He turned to her. "I... that is, in case... We won't get to say what we might wanna say once we're with your intended, so I wanted to say now that..."

She smiled, shaking her head. "You don't need to. I understand."

"I don't think you do."

Her shoulders raised in a slight shrug. "Maybe it's best to leave things where they are, then. Besides, I have a wedding to get to." Before there was the chance to say anything more, she took the reins and tapped them to the horses' backs to send them on their way.

He'd lost his chance. There would never be another moment so perfect.

It was for the best, wasn't it? The woman wanted to get down there, meet up with her fiancé and get married, fast. He couldn't blame her. Mark Furnish offered everything a man such as himself could never dream of giving her.

Including a good, stable father for her child.

He could only follow her and hope they kept their stories straight when it came time to collect his payment. And that Furnish would believe them.

He had no reason not to, so far as Jed was concerned. There was no one to contradict their story, and he was delivering Melissa without so much as a scratch on her. If that wasn't a gesture of good faith, he didn't know what was.

The money was as good as his. He tried to picture it in his head, tried to imagine the land and stock he'd purchase for himself. So long as he got the chance to work on the land again, to be part of it instead of just traveling over it. To watch a herd move together as one and know that sense of pride again, pride that he'd had a hand in bringing them up, in making them what they were. Something real, something honest.

He'd had enough of the other life, his life up to that point. He would never take again. He would give, instead, and maybe even like himself a little better when his head touched his pillow at the end of a long day.

It was her. She was the reason these thoughts—so unusual for him—had run through his head ever since he knew he loved her. Especially since that kiss.

The best kiss he'd ever had, without a doubt. A kiss that might easily have turned into something more—God knew he'd wanted her, aching so bad he could've sworn he was about to bust through his trousers. It had almost hurt, truly hurt, when he'd turned away from her.

Because she'd wanted it, too, which made the refusing doubly hard.

She was not his to take.

He would no longer take from other men that which was not his for the taking.

So one of them had to be stronger, and it had turned out to be him. The ache of pent-up longing might have kept him up through the night if his troubled thoughts hadn't. Thoughts of her, of Jasper, of what life might look like if he forgave himself for that terrible day and moved on with things.

He had never once considered what Jasper would think of the way his big brother's life turned out. The very idea filled him with shame. He'd been a hero to the boy and look how things had changed. Maybe it was the easy way out, living as he had once the war ended, and he had no home to go back to.

For that alone, he would have remembered her forever and thanked her whenever something good came into his life.

After their kiss, he would always wonder what might have come of them if she wasn't already married to one man and promised to another. Just his luck, finding the woman who just might be perfect for him and knowing she was so far beyond his reach.

Even then, she drove the wagon in silence, like he wasn't even there. Head high, shoulders squared, she might just as well have been riding at the head of a parade. She could have worn a crown on that head of hers. A woman who'd seen everything she'd seen, suffered as she had suffered, but still had a tender heart.

How rare she was.

Mark Furnish had better know how good he had it.

Then again, Jed reflected with a spiteful sneer, he would

never know if Melissa was happy or treated well. He'd be far away. He'd have to put a mountain between them, maybe even a few thousand miles, before he could trust himself to leave her be.

They rode past a few shacks on the outskirts of town on a street marked "William," the noisy train shed to their left, before turning left onto the wide street marked "Carson." This was where everything happened. They passed the Carson City Mint, where several men stopped to speak on their way to begin the day's work. Beyond that was a mercantile, a saloon, a bank.

They attracted no attention, mainly because there was so much going on. People walking, riding, driving buggies. Washing the windows of the stores, sweeping the boards of the sidewalks. Carts full of goods—probably from the freight that had just pulled in—pulled by teams of oxen.

There was nothing so interesting about a man and a woman simply driving down the city's thoroughfare. Nothing at all.

She looked over at him. "I suppose I should check at the Butterfield office, as that was where I was supposed to be coming through."

He nodded, looking around. "I'd better hang back." For word of the robbery would surely have reached the office, and maybe a description of him. He'd covered his face, but there was never any telling with such matters.

"Meet me in front of the dressmaker's across the way?" she asked, looking down at herself. "I might be able to charge something suitable in Mr. Furnish's name. I don't feel like I can see him looking this way—and between the two of us, I might have eaten my way out of ever fitting into my dress again."

He managed to stifle a chuckle. Yes, she had quite an appetite, but there was good reason for it. And he wouldn't have liked to see her in that rag again—stained around the hem and cuffs, terribly frayed, worn almost clear through at the elbows.

Dressed as a man was not a better option. She might have done well with a bath, too, but he held his tongue and merely nodded in agreement.

The less he said, the better. He no longer trusted himself. For something was squeezing his heart, like a pair of iron shackles tightening with every passing minute. Every minute closer to saying goodbye.

There was no telling what might pour out of his mouth, or how much of a damned fool he might make of himself. Better to stay quiet, then.

Though he felt like a true fool coming to a stop in front of the dressmaker's shop, tying the reins to the post running along the plank sidewalk. Two frilly things sat in the window, full of ruffles and lace. It made a man feel downright womanish to be seen standing nearby.

Yet he couldn't help imagining Melissa in one of them.

Or in nothing at all.

Blowing out a long, slow breath, he decided to think on other things. A handsome carriage, black leather, came rolling down the street on wheels with red spokes. A dandy, he decided. Someone who'd paid their way out of the draft.

A weathered old woman in a brown dress riding astride a speckled mare, her white-streaked black hair in two braids hanging down to her waist. She spat tobacco juice on the ground without so much as a glance in either direction to see whether anyone noticed. Jed grinned. She'd be somebody he'd like to speak with.

After a while, watching the people come and go grew on his nerves. What was taking her so long? Was there trouble? His body tightened, like a coiled spring ready to burst forth. Maybe he ought not to have tied the wagon off, after all.

He was three paces from it when a trio of men galloped down Carson Street out of the eastern end of town, opposite the way he rode in with Melissa. Two of them were dressed in clothing he recognized right off as those of a ranch hand—rough, worn trousers, scuffed boots, sweat-stained hats.

The third, however, wore a rather fine suit of dark gray, a white shirt, black boots. His hat was black, too, making as was the black hair hanging in a lock over his forehead and spread.

His horse was fine, a chestnut brown mustang he must've had a hell of a time breaking. It tossed its proud head as its rider dismounted and hurried into the office where Melissa had intended to check—

"Oh." It came out of him in a gust, like somebody hit him square in the belly and knocked out all his wind.

That could only be Mark Furnish, come to claim his bride.

19

M elissa glanced out the window of the stagecoach office, wishing she could speak to Jed and explain what she'd found out.

Namely that her fiancé had been staying at the only hotel in town ever since she hadn't arrived on the coach two weeks earlier. He'd haunted the office every day, waiting for some word of what came of her after the robbery, demanding the sheriff contact other lawmen in Nevada, Texas, even the Colorado Territory in search of her. Half the town was all but holding vigils to pray for her safe arrival.

And she'd merely wanted a quick ceremony and even quicker bedding.

Meanwhile, Jed waited within her line of sight, unaware of the nightmare unfolding before her. She did not wish for fame, short-lived though it might be. She did not wish for anything but a safe place to rest her head and a good life for her baby.

At least, that had been all she'd wished for prior to making Jed's acquaintance.

Now, knowing how her fiancé had suffered while awaiting her arrival—knowing already how she'd planned to lie to him about the baby, about her marriage, even about Jed's true identity—was a knife twisting in her chest.

When a tall, handsome man in fine clothes burst through the door, she knew it could only be one person. He removed his hat, revealing dark hair and a strikingly handsome face.

"Melissa?" He marched across the front office, the heels of his boots clicking smartly against the wood floor, stopping just short of taking her in his arms. She knew from the way he held his body that he longed to, but held himself back for propriety's sake.

"Yes, I am. I'm sorry to be so late," she blushed, wishing for all the world there wasn't so much sincerity in his shockingly blue eyes.

He took her hands—his were large, calloused, like Jed's. Why was she thinking about Jed? Even at barely more than a few moments acquaintance, the differences between the two men were plain.

"It was through no fault of your own," Mark smiled. "I am simply relieved to have you here, at last. How did you manage it? No, no." He shook his head, suddenly serious. "There is more than enough time to talk it over during our ride to the ranch. And I'm sure you're too tired, and the whole ordeal is too fresh for you to wish to relive it right this minute."

She nodded, mute in the shadow of his expansive, energetic personality. How much of his attitude was sheer relief and how much was Mark Furnish?

The last thing she took note of on leaving the dusty, cluttered office was the scowl on the face of the man who ran the place. He wanted all the details of her kidnapping and was disappointed at not hearing them.

Mark knew it, too. "I figured on you not wishing to go through your story in the presence of a gossip like Dan Learner," he murmured, even winking as he took her arm upon stepping outside.

"You are too right," she grinned, even as her eyes searched the street for Jed. When she caught his gaze, a lump formed in her throat.

Mark followed the direction of her stare. "Who is that man?"

It was time to begin one of the biggest lies she would ever tell—funny how all of her lies would be directed at the same man. "He is the one who rescued me when I might just as well have died out on the plains," she explained. "When I escaped the bandits, I rode as hard and fast as I could, but both I and the horse collapsed from exhaustion after a spell. I knew not where I was, I had no money or food. He saved my life and agreed to accompany me to Carson City, so I might arrive safely."

Would he believe it? He had no reason not to. As far as

he was concerned, his mail-order bride was an honest woman.

Mark wasted no time waving Jed across the street. It was better for her to allow them to work things out on their own, she decided, as telling more lies to a man who seemed so decent made her feel very small and despicable. She stepped back a bit, wishing she might fade completely away.

Nothing was the way it was supposed to be. Nothing at all.

She was not supposed to like Jed after what he'd done. She was certainly not supposed to love him or dread the thought of being away from him. She wasn't supposed to fear for him as he crossed the street, hoping with all her heart he got his money and was able to start a new, honest life for himself.

Mark thrust out his hand when Jed reached them. "Mark Furnish. I owe you a great debt of gratitude."

Jed shook his hand. "Jed Cunningham."

"I can't possibly repay you for what you've done, but I can try," Mark smiled. "Come with us to the ranch, where I'll make sure to settle accounts with you. You ought to get some rest and a few hearty meals in your stomach before you go on your way, too."

"Oh. That would be..." Jed looked to her for help, which she was far too overwhelmed to offer. "That would be right kind of you."

"Wonderful. We'd better be off, then—I sent one of my men to rent a buggy from the livery, as I'm sure you would rather not ride another mile in discomfort if you could help it."

Melissa smiled. "You've thought of everything, it seems. I... thought we would be married right away, though."

He patted her arm. "This is hardly the way to do it, wouldn't you agree? You look as though what you're most in need of is a bath, a meal, and a long sleep. I can send for the preacher and have him come to the ranch—he knows you're expected. Many people know you were due to arrive."

"Yes, so I heard." She forced a fainthearted smile.

A black buggy pulled up, hitched to a pair of white stallions. Mark could afford such a handsome rig. He helped her inside and took the reins while two other men mounted their horses and rode alongside Jed and the wagon.

They followed Carson Street out of town and kept going straight. Melissa tried to settle back against the leather seat. It was the most luxurious thing she'd ever sat upon, worlds away from the wooden bench of the stagecoach.

If only she could enjoy it with her whole heart.

Mark smiled a bit shyly. "I can't tell you how much I admire your courage. From what I've heard, those bandits were a tough sort, indeed."

"That they were." The less she spoke of them, the better. She folded her hands to keep them from shaking and willed herself not to cast too many looks outside the buggy, to where Jed rode.

"It speaks well to the way you'll manage ranch life," he continued. "My greatest concern was that my wife be suited to the land, the busyness, and occasional hardship. That she be able to fend for herself when I'm out with the men."

"I'm glad to know you're pleased with me." That would be a tremendous first, knowing she impressed and pleased a man. She certainly never had before.

"Now that we're somewhat more alone," he murmured, "I must say I'm pleased to find how pretty you are, too."

Her cheeks flushed. "Thank you. I don't feel that way at the moment."

"Some ladies are just pretty no matter the state they're in. You can smear dirt on them and dress them in rags—or, as in your case, a man's shirt and trousers—and they're lovely."

He ought to have seen her during her girlhood, as that had been her normal state.

She searched for something else to speak about. He was to be her husband, after all, and she ought to get used to making conversation with him. "I heard from the gentleman in the stagecoach office that you stayed in town for two weeks. Is that so?"

"It is."

"How did you manage? When you wrote to me, you spoke of how busy ranch life is."

He nodded. "True, which is why two of my hands came out to visit me every day in order to keep me up-to-date on ranch business. They would leave in the afternoon, while two more would come in the evening if need be. So on and so forth until you arrived."

"You did all of that for me?"

He smiled that sweet, shy smile again. "How could I remain at the ranch, so far from town, when I didn't know where you were? I had to do everything in my power to locate you. I was not aware of your escort, naturally."

"Naturally," she whispered, blushing again but not for the same reason as before.

She ventured a look outside. Just one, just to check on him. Jed rode beside them, keeping to himself rather than speaking to the pair of ranch hands who flanked him. What was he thinking?

"If it pleases you, we can hold the wedding tomorrow morning," Mark offered.

"That will do nicely." She hardly heard the words coming from her mouth over the racing of her heart. She was so close to having everything she'd prayed for.

How cruel, then, that she had no desire for the decent, hardworking man who'd spent two weeks striving to locate her. And she still had no choice but to lie.

In Boston, she'd never imagined there being other types of misery than her own. Poverty, starvation, abuse—she had suffered them while imagining there could be nothing worse.

She'd never known the suffering of taking advantage of a good man—and her suffering had only begun. She'd known Mark for an entire thirty minutes, and already she longed to apologize.

It was easy to allow him to do the talking as they rolled along the dusty road. While he was not a braggart, his pride was evident. "My father bought the land years ago, when I was but a baby in my mother's arms."

"Where did you come from?"

"St. Louis. My father was in business out there, and some of his firm's clients owned land out here and in Texas. He got the itch, I suppose you might say. Fell in love with the notion of no longer working for a boss, behind a desk, in the cramped city. Stories about the wide, open spaces and blue sky as far as the eye could see." There was more than a little wryness in the way he chuckled at this.

"Is that not the truth of it, then?"

"You tell me, Melissa. You're the one who just made a harrowing journey on horseback from—where was it they took you? North Texas?"

"Somewhere near there, yes. And I see what you mean. He was unprepared for the harshness of it."

He nodded. "You're perceptive. Yes. That's why I was certain to be honest with you when I wrote. I would not wish to mislead you on the way life is out here."

"Was your father unhappy with his decision?"

"Oh, not at all—he simply took time to adjust his expectations. This land is certainly a heaven sometimes, but it's much more a hell at others." He cast a worried look her way. "Pardon my language."

She barely stopped herself from laughing. "I have heard much worse." Had she ever. The word "hell" was the very least of them and something her husband had screamed on a daily basis.

It was the memory of him and of what he would have

done to her baby that kept Melissa in the buggy, silently riding beside her intended. When she reconsidered the situation with John Carter in mind, her lies seemed less important with every turn of the big wheels.

"Our nearest neighbors are twenty miles from the house," Mark informed her with an apologetic smile. "Though they are good friends, and I'm certain you'll get along well with Lena Belton."

"Is she the rancher's wife?"

"Sister," he explained. "Ryan and Lena lost their parents several years back. Ryan has been like a brother to me— rode out to town several times these past two weeks, checking on your situation. I know they'll be anxious to meet you tomorrow."

Tomorrow. It would all be settled, everything put to rest. She would have nothing more to fear. Once she was married—really, truly married, married without question or doubt—she might breathe more easily.

Suddenly, she found herself gasping for air. Panic? She thought not, as she knew panic too well to mistake it for anything else.

"Are you well? Should we stop?"

So attentive, so eager to please her. Never had a man treated her this way.

Except for Jed.

She shook her head. "No, please. I am eager to see the ranch, and I'm sure you would like to arrive. I'm somewhat overwhelmed, is all."

He took the liberty of patting her hand. "You need not

be overwhelmed. Just be yourself, as you have so charmingly done so far. As for the ranch?" His smile widened. "We're already here."

She blinked hard, looking about herself. There was nothing as far as the eye could see but grass and flat land. There were foothills in the distance, taller peaks somewhat further off. Blue sky, billowing clouds.

"We're on the ranch?" she asked, feeling immensely stupid.

"We are. Everything you see here, to the foothills in the east, is ours. Furnish land." For one brief, heartbreaking moment, she thought he might take her hand. He did not, but again she sensed his desire to extend further intimacy.

Could it be that her absence created a deeper feeling in him than there should have been? He'd spent two weeks waiting, worrying, asking others to help find her. Perhaps this had endeared her to him.

She hoped it was nothing more than imagination causing her to think along these lines.

Once the house came into view, there was nothing to do but admire its beauty. "That's the house?" she gasped, sitting forward on the leather seat, straining for a better look over the tops of the horses' heads. It was a mansion, plain and simple, the most elegant one she'd ever seen. Even more impressive than the fine houses she'd admired in Boston—the houses she knew she would never step foot inside.

This house would be hers. All four floors of it, white brick, the fourth-floor windows jutting out from a gray slate-tiled roof which rose high and sloped downward. A deep porch wrapped around the first floor, shaded by sycamore trees.

"I had it built three years ago in the latest style," he explained. "With a wife in mind, you see. It's always been important for me to find a wife and have children to pass the ranch down to. I didn't think a lady would want to live in the smaller, rather knockabout place that used to pass as the main house. I've since handed that home off to my overseer."

He pointed to the left, beyond the white fence which surrounded the great house, to a smaller house Melissa would have been delighted to call her own. A modest two floors rather than four, wooden shingles covering the walls and roof, a porch with a flower garden in front.

It spoke to her heart in a way the larger house did not.

Even so, this was not what her intended would wish to hear. "I'm greatly impressed," she admitted with a soft laugh. "I'm afraid I might become lost in such a grand house!"

"You'll have plenty of help." He pulled the buggy to a stop and set the brake before alighting, hurrying to her side that he might help her down. Memories of Mr. Lang and his pocket watch flashed before her, but that was all it was. A memory. Something she'd once lived through.

This was her new life.

"Come on inside," Mark beckoned, waving for Jed to join them. "You'll want to freshen up, I reckon."

Jed dismounted, handing the reins off to one of the

ranch hands who led the horses to the stable. He looked up at the house, tipping back the brim of his hat to take in the entire sight.

"Quite a place," he observed, then caught Melissa's eye. "Quite a place."

And there he was in his dirty clothing, his ragged boots. He could never give her something like the mansion which stood before them.

She could never tell him she didn't want it or anything like it, that she never had.

20

T his was precisely what he didn't need.

Dinner in the home of the man whose money he planned to take.

God truly had to possess a sense of humor, of that Jed was certain as he bathed in a metal washtub brought specially to his room and filled just for him.

His room. The man had offered him a room. And not with the ranch hands, in one of the small bunkhouses they lived on along the outskirts of Furnish land. In the big house.

He had never been so embarrassed by another man's generosity before, and it was nobody's fault but his. Mark Furnish merely wished to extend kindness to the man he believed had saved his fiancée's life. If Jed had been in his place, he'd have done the same.

For nothing was too good when it came to Melissa.

If she were his, he'd have showered her savior with gold

and promises of anything he wanted in the world short of his very life.

The woman was that special. Her safety was that precious.

He sank low in the tub, briefly considering going under and never coming up. She belonged to another man. She would never be his. He could never offer her half of what Furnish could. And she deserved this, all of it and more. After what she'd been through, she deserved the world.

He'd give it to her if he could. He'd spend the rest of his life trying to, for damn sure.

"What a fool," he muttered, staring up at the plaster ceiling. There were no cracks. It was that new. There had never been a mistress there. She would be the first.

He imagined them having guests, using the house's many bedrooms to entertain friends and important people coming through Carson City. Melissa might not have been schooled in the finer arts, the things great ladies were supposed to be schooled in when he was growing up, but she could learn.

The woman had taught herself to read, and he imagined it was sometimes with one eye swollen shut.

Yes, she could learn anything, and she'd be a dazzling sight to see once she took her place in Carson City society. He imagined the sort of gowns her husband could buy for her, the jewels at her throat and ears, wrists and fingers.

None of it would be as dazzling as the woman herself, with that tinkling laugh of hers, that sharp wit. Many would be the man who'd fall in love with her.

He knew how easy it was to do, after all. Too well.

A knock at the door told him his clothing had been dropped off after washing and drying—the blazing sun had done wonders, he noted when he opened the door to find them neatly folded on a chair just outside. The Furnish household ran smoothly, even without a woman to oversee things.

Within a single day, that woman would be Melissa.

He closed the door again and leaned against it, forehead on his arm, eyes closed. How was he supposed to get her out of his head and his heart?

There was no choice but to leave after supper, was all. Furnish's insistence that he stay was too much to refuse, but he'd make it clear to the man that he had things to do once the meal was finished. It was time to move on, away from her and the sight of her dancing eyes, her soft lips, the curve of her cheek, the dimples when she smiled.

He could not see her on her wedding day. He was a strong man, God knew, but there were limits to any man's control.

Once he'd shaved and dressed—clean clothes had never felt so good, and it had been ages since he'd rested in a real bathtub—he traced the steps he'd taken upon entering the house, walking down a carpeted hall and down a wide set of stairs which left him in the entry hall.

To the right of the front door was a drawing room, to the left was a study. Everything still felt fresh, new. Unlived in. Like the owner had waited for his wife before he started living in the place.

There was something strangely touching about the whole thing, really.

He wished it wasn't so, since hating the man would've made things a hell of a lot easier.

As if he heard Jed's thoughts about him, Mark stepped out of the study. "Jed." He nodded. "Are you a whiskey man?"

"I grew up in Texas."

Mark's laugh rang through the hall. "I'll take that as a yes. Come. Join me for a drink—a celebration, if you will."

Damn it, why did he have to be so generous and likable? "Thank you, sir. It's been a long time since I had a good glass of whiskey."

"Please, don't call me sir. It's Mark. And I only buy the best."

Jed followed him into the handsome room, its walls paneled in the same fine, shining oak as the floor. Books lined the wall opposite the windows, and the desk was a clutter of ledger books and purchase orders.

A pair of high-backed chairs sat facing each other in front of a fireplace decorated in marble. Between them was a small table holding a decanter and two glasses. "Please. Take a load off," Mark invited, taking one of the chairs for himself.

Jed looked around, whistling through his teeth. "Yours is surely the most impressive ranch I've ever seen, Mark. And the most impressive house by far."

"You've seen a lot of ranches, then?" Mark poured a

healthy glug of amber liquid into two glasses, passing one to Jed before raising his own in a silent toast.

"Oh, sure. I grew up on one, in fact. Spent the first sixteen years of my life there."

"You don't say."

Jed nodded, his eyes widening at the smooth whiskey when it hit his lips. A man could get used to this sort of life. "Ours was a modest outfit, nothing like this. Twenty-thousand acres, roughly five-hundred head."

"Still sizable," Mark allowed. Men in his position could afford to be generous that way. They could afford a great many things, such as the finest whiskey Jed had ever tasted.

"I was always rather proud of it," Jed admitted, looking down into the glass. "Of course, I was a boy who only thought he was a man."

"Much as all of us were at that age, I reckon."

"I reckon so."

"Did you have many responsibilities there, on the ranch?"

"Sure. My pa groomed me to take over."

"But you didn't."

"I did not."

Mark pursed his lips. "It isn't fair of me to pry, of course."

Jed shifted in the chair, stretching his legs. "There was an accident, and my father and I had a falling out over it. The war came. By the time I got up the nerve to write home, both of my parents were dead, and the ranch split up, sold off."

"I'm very sorry to hear that—for you, and for what your father built. It's never easy, seeing the things somebody worked hard for just slip away. I could have faced that very reality here, to be honest with you."

Jed frowned. "Pardon my saying, but the Furnish name has been a big damn deal since I was old enough to know what made boys and girls so different."

Mark laughed as he poured himself another drink. "I don't normally drink this much so early in the evening, but this is a celebration. And to address your observation, the name is indeed well-known and even respected. But things might have easily gone south when my father passed on. He groomed me, too, but he didn't plan on succumbing so soon—doctor always told him to learn to cool his temper, said it would be the death of him one day. And it was, I'm sorry to say."

"You didn't expect to take over when you did."

"That's the long and short of it. I scrambled for a long while but managed to stay afloat and continue to grow the name and the ranch. My foreman was a great help, but he's getting on in years and wishes to rest for the rest of his years. It's quite a problem, though he taught me a great deal about the business side of the operation." He shrugged. "I always cared more for the roping and riding, myself."

"Being on the land," Jed agreed, remembering how it felt to be out among the cattle.

"We are of the same mind." They raised their glasses to each other before draining them.

A knock at the open door, which both men turned at

the sound of. Thanks to the whiskey, Jed was feeling better than he had in a long time. It was almost possible to forget the only woman he'd ever loved was upstairs, getting ready for supper the night before her wedding.

Almost.

"Pardon me, Mark." A ranch hand stood in the doorway, nodding mute acknowledgment of their guest.

"Yes, Davey?"

"There's a man outside, saying he needs to speak to you. Saying it's real important, that he wants to come in. Some of the others managed to hold him off, but he's pretty serious about getting to you."

"What's this about?" Mark stood, buttoned his waistcoat. "I'll come with you outside rather than allowing him in."

Jed got up to join him, just in case there was trouble and he needed the extra help. Why in the hell did he care? Damn it, he liked the man far too much. At least he could rest easy knowing Melissa would be with a good, honest fellow.

Outside, surrounded by four rather surly looking hands, was a tall, thick-shouldered man with raven-black hair and hard, dark eyes which shifted back and forth as he sized up the men around him. The way he held himself told Jed he was ready for a fight.

He might even be looking for one.

Jed disliked him intensely even before he stepped over the threshold, a few paces behind the owner of the house.

"What can I help you with?" Mark asked, hands on hips as he looked down at the man before him.

"I've come to collect what's mine. I believe you'll want to hear what I have to say." He lifted his chin, a strangely triumphant smile on his face. "In fact, I know you will. You need to know who it is you think you're about to take as your wife."

Just like that, it was all clear.

How had he?

How was it possible?

At the same time, light footsteps rang out behind him, coming closer. No. It couldn't be. This was all going to explode into something more terrible than anything he could imagine.

Jed turned, intent on stopping her from coming out.

Desperate to stop her.

"Don't," he managed to say, a second before her husband saw her.

"Melissa." John spat the name out as though it were a curse. "It's been a long time, wife."

"Wife?" Mark asked.

Melissa's eyes widened into two horrified, panicked orbs. Her lovely face shifted into a mask of terror.

"That's what I said." John jabbed a finger in Jed's direction, sneering. "And that's the man who kidnapped her from the stagecoach."

21

I t couldn't be happening. It couldn't possibly be happening. She must have fallen asleep in that big, soft feather bed upstairs, after taking the longest bath she'd ever enjoyed.

She must have been dreaming this. Her inner thoughts were still tied up in John Carter and his evil, vicious ways. She could not stop dreaming about him.

But that did not mean he truly stood before her in the front yard of what was soon to be her home, for that would be impossible. There was no earthly way he could have found her.

Yet when she blinked hard, a gesture which normally woke her when she was aware of a nightmare and wished to escape, nothing happened. She remained in the front hall, just inside the door, still looking out at the man who could not possibly be there.

But he was. And he laughed that same nasty laugh at the sight of her dismay.

"There she is. The woman I traveled all this way to find." John shook his head, then glanced at Mark from the corner of his eye. "I wouldn't blame you if you killed her for this—or the man who came with her."

"Wait just a minute." Mark stepped between them, blessedly blocking John from her view. "What is this all about? Who are you?"

"John Carter, of Boston, Massachusetts. That woman has been my wife for a year. And have you forgotten that the man she's with is the one who kidnapped her? I suggest you get him under your control before he pulls out a pistol."

Mark turned, a pained look on his face. "Is this true?"

When Jed didn't answer quickly enough, Mark nodded to his men. "Take him inside. Tie him to a chair in the study, make certain he's disarmed."

Words of dismay, words of defense, pleas and bargains came to Melissa's mind, but none of them would form on her deadened tongue. Something about the presence of that evil man silenced her. All of the daring she'd built up over the weeks of travel dissolved like a lump of sugar in a cup of tea.

She could only watch helplessly as the men who'd only just surrounded John enclosed Jed instead. They all but carried him into the house, muttering amongst themselves in angry tones.

He did not look at her.

Mark met her gaze instead. "Come inside. I want to have this out." He took her elbow before looking over his shoulder. "You, too. Just remember you are a guest in my house, sir."

Melissa was careful to keep her eyes low, on the floor, away from the brute she'd lost a year of her life to.

How had he found her, the devil? Only he would go to such lengths. Mark's hand was firm, gripping her tightly as he led her to the study where Jed was already tied to a chair at his wrists and ankles.

What did he think of her? And of the weeks he'd spent waiting? She could never make it up to him.

"Now." Mark deposited her beside his desk—he was not rough, but the gentleness he'd shown her up until now had gone away—before sitting behind it in a leather chair. "What is this really all about? I would ask you to explain yourself, sir."

"I am not the one who needs to explain," John spat, throwing his head back in a gesture of pride Melissa had seen many times before. "She is, as well as the thief who brought her here."

"What makes you call him a thief?" Mark looked to Jed, who sat straight in the chair.

Jed did not cower, did not look elsewhere or even appear apologetic. In fact, he looked furious.

He glared at John with such intensity, it was a wonder her husband did not burst into flame. John, naturally, was unaware of this or simply did not care.

"His name is Jed, is it not?" he asked, arching one heavy,

black eyebrow. "One of the men who survived that terrible robbery heard one of the robbers refer to the man who rode off with my wife as Jed."

Of course, they had. The fools. They weren't supposed to use anyone's name—and of all the names they could have shared, it was Jed's.

Mark frowned, the muscles in his jaw jumping as he studied Jed. "Have you anything to say for yourself?"

"What could he possibly have to say?" John laughed.

"I don't recall asking you, sir." Mark's eyes reflected the hardness in his voice. "I was speaking to Jed."

For the first time, John appeared to back down. For once, he was not the strongest man in the room. Mark Furnish might have appeared gentle and kind on the surface—and perhaps he was—but beneath that was a core of steel.

If nothing came of this but the chance to see him cut down to size, it would be worthwhile.

Jed glared at John. "I was one of the men who robbed the stagecoach."

Melissa's heart sank, both for him and for Mark.

"Why did you go to the trouble of bringing Melissa here?" Mark asked.

"Because she asked me for help. My men died or ran off, leaving only me. I had no wish to continue in the vein I'd started in and offered to let her go—but rather than allow her to wander alone with no money and no sense of where she was, I agreed to escort her here."

"Such a gentleman," John snorted.

"You're one to talk," Jed fired back, his hands working, his arms straining against the rope restraints. "I ought to tear your head off for the things you've done to her. Why do you think she went to this trouble? Because she adored being your wife?" Jed snarled in laughter. "Your wife. More like something to kick around like a stray dog."

"Wait, wait." Mark raised his voice over the others as he stood. "I'm the one asking questions, and this is still my house. I would thank you both to remain quiet unless you're asked to speak."

John threw back his broad shoulders. "This is ridiculous, and I refuse to play nice in front of these two simply because you told me to do so. I'm not a child. I'm a man who is claiming what's his."

"Do you have proof of that claim?" Mark asked.

John blinked. "Do I what?"

"Have proof that she's your wife. Do you have a marriage certificate I can review?"

Melissa met John's eyes for the first time since he'd arrived, her spine stiffening as she found her voice. "I would like to see it, too, since I never have."

"Shut up," he snarled, his vicious nature bubbling to the surface—as she'd known it would the moment they shared words.

"Do not speak to her that way," Mark warned. "Your own wife has never seen proof of your marriage?"

"She wears the ring I gave her," John pointed out. "And it was good enough for her to live under my roof, supported by me when her family didn't have money or food enough to keep her."

His thin mouth curved into a nasty smile then, as he looked her up and down. She knew that smile. It was the smile he wore before he was about to land a terrible blow. He'd once knocked her to the floor with a single slap to her face after smiling that way.

Just the sight of it made her fear she might lose her water there in the middle of the room.

"Not to mention the fact that she's carrying my child," he added, still smiling.

The room went silent. Even the ranch hands lingering in the corner froze in place as though time itself had stopped in the face of this devastating announcement.

How did he know? How had he always managed to remain a step ahead of her?

Mark, bless him, sat down with a thud. "Come again?"

"She's carrying a child. My child. I suspect she would have pretended it was yours," John chuckled. "You owe me quite a lot, Mr. Furnish. I've spared you a great deal of embarrassment."

"How did you know?" she whispered. She needed to understand, regardless of the fact that none of it mattered.

"Did you truly believe Dr. Hawkins would remain silent simply because you asked him to?" John murmured, his head tilted to the side. "Did you think he would refuse to tell a husband, a father-to-be, of his wife's condition after hearing she'd run away? That child is mine, and you are mine, and as such, I deserve to know where you are and what you've done. I've crossed the country in search of you after the station master told me he'd seen you board a train to St. Louis. After that, I followed the route the stagecoach took and heard of the robbery. I followed you all the way out here—but I guess I made better time, since I waited in town three days for you to arrive."

He turned to Mark. "It was because of you that I knew I'd hit the right place. You were waiting for your bride-to-be, who was captured in a robbery. I admit, I was stunned —I still didn't know then that she'd planned to wed, but it made sense once I got over the shock of it. Yes, sir. She intended to make fools of us both."

"What of the fool you made of me?" she asked, gripping the side of the desk for support. With the men around, she could finally ask what had weighed on her since three days after their supposed wedding. "You granted me a pitiful excuse for a wedding which might not even have been legal. You waited three days before the beatings began."

"Beatings," he sniffed, shaking his head.

She opened her mouth, pointing inside. "You knocked out three of my teeth when I burned your toast on the fourth morning of our married life. Do you remember?" She touched the back of her head. "There will always be a scar from the time you struck me, and I fell against the bedpost. There are stormy days when I cannot use my right arm very well. Do you remember dislocating my shoulder?"

"I refuse to listen to any more of this," John growled, leaning over the desk.

"I, for one, would like to hear it," Mark said, standing by her side.

This bolstered her even further. "You call yourself a husband when you speak of me as though I was nothing but property you bought one day. You would treat your child the same if you even allowed it to be born, if you managed to keep from beating it out of me. Yes. I came out here to make a new life for my child, and I would have lied to this good, kind man just to make sure my baby and I had a decent place to live and security, which we would never have gotten if I stayed with you. I've finally met good men, honest men who don't believe in hurting women to make themselves feel strong, and you are nothing compared to them. You are weak and cowardly, and I hate you."

He lunged for her before she had the chance to duck him, his massive hand making contact with the side of her head hard enough to send stars dancing in front of her eyes. She fell against the desk and slid to the floor.

A burst of shouts came from all sides as John took a handful of her hair and pulled her to her knees. She gripped his wrist in an effort to prevent him from tearing her hair clean out, Jed's screams and curses filling her head.

"Let go of her!" Mark shouted. "You will not do this!" He scuffled with John, who would not release her. John pushed him away before pulling his arm back to strike her again—this time, his hand was curled into a fist.

"I'll kill the bitch if I damn well choose!" John roared over the shouts and warnings all around him.

Melissa crossed her arms over her head, bracing herself for the blow.

The crack of a gunshot startled a yelp from her throat. The smell of gunpowder filled the air, all but choking her.

The hand in her hair relaxed. Released.

John's powerful body fell to the floor, powerful no more.

Melissa blinked rapidly, one hand against the side of her face where a bruise would most certainly form.

At first, she couldn't believe what she saw. A red rose blooming against the white of John's shirt, over his chest. His dark eyes, no longer hard and mean but wide, unblinking.

Unseeing.

She looked up at the hand extended to her. Mark's hand.

In the other was the still-smoking pistol he'd used to shoot her husband dead.

"You were right about one thing," he growled on helping her to her feet. "I cannot abide a man who would hurt a woman."

22

J ed was certain he'd never been so surprised.

Or relieved.

Or envious, as he'd wanted to be the one to take the man down.

"Untie him," Mark ordered his men as Jed comforted Melissa, who trembled and turned her face from her dead husband. Jed had wasted no time in leaping from the chair and going to her.

She turned to him, leaned against his chest, allowed him to enfold her in his arms. "I wanted to be the one to do it," he murmured in her ear, holding her as tight as she would let him.

"I know," she mumbled against his chest.

Out of the corner of his eye, Jed caught Mark's perceptive gaze, and his sigh as he understood and took a step away from them.

He turned to the men. "I suppose there'll be an inquest.

Somebody better ride for Doc Perkins, not that it'll do this scoundrel much good."

"You won't get in trouble, will you?" Melissa asked, pulling away from Jed and taking Mark's arm.

He patted her hand. "I have several witnesses including yourself. It was done in your defense."

"I don't know how to thank you."

"You don't need to." He nodded to another of the men. "Please head down to the ice house and fetch some for Melissa's cheek, would you? And I believe we ought to get you out of here, away from this bloody mess."

He turned to Melissa, frowning. "Maybe you ought to lie down and rest until we're certain you're well. Doc Perkins can come up and take a look at you when he arrives." He glanced down at her stomach before quickly turning his eyes away.

She took his meaning. "Yes, I think I ought to. Are you... sure you don't mind? It's all right if I do?"

His eyebrows lifted in silent question—but this, too, he understood. "If you mean, would I turn away a woman in a delicate condition because she was desperate to escape an animal like that, the answer is no. I would never do any such thing. When Seth returns with the ice, you lie down and take care of yourself."

She did just that, casting one more look over her shoulder to where Jed stood before climbing the stairs. He was careful to maintain a smile until she was out of sight.

He looked at Mark.

Mark looked at him.

"I believe we could both use another drink," he decided, waving Jed into the drawing room across from the study. "Good thing I keep a supply handy. Not that I'm too overly fond of it, mind you, but I believe in having it close at hand for my guests, wherever they happen to be in the house."

Jed followed him with caution. What was this? Some sort of game? He watched as Mark went to a cabinet and withdrew another decanter, another pair of glasses.

When he turned to hand one of them to Jed, it was time to speak. "What do you intend to do now? What is this all about?"

Mark blinked, then nodded. "Right. Of course. You want to know what I think about what that nasty bastard said before I shot him."

"A good shot," Jed observed.

"I'm a dead eye when it counts," Mark muttered before draining half the whiskey in the glass. He took a slow breath after swallowing, steadying himself. Jed noticed for the first time how his hands shook slightly, as though reality was setting in.

"But what of what he said? I won't lie to you anymore. I did kidnap Melissa with the intention of ransoming her to you."

"Why did you do that?"

The frankness of the question and the curiosity in Mark's voice surprised him, made it difficult to answer right away. "I—I hoped to use it to buy some land for myself. The money, I mean."

"You made a career of robbing stagecoaches before this last robbery, I assume." He perched on a windowsill in the vast, airy room, somehow managing to look casual. As though he shot men in his home every day.

Jed was careful to hold his gaze, to return Mark's frankness. "I did. For several years."

"Because you no longer had a home to go to?"

"That's a large part of it, yes. I needed money. I needed a way to live. I had no skills outside ranching and, well, I feared that word of the accident at my pa's ranch had gotten around. There was no one to write to for references, as everyone had scattered to the four winds."

"What was this accident all about? Can you tell me?"

And so, Jed told him in the briefest, simplest way he could of the accident which claimed his brother's life. After having shared with Melissa, it became easier to speak of it. Yet another thing he could thank her for.

Mark sat back, his head against the window frame. "You're telling me the whole truth, as it occurred?"

"Yes, sir."

"Mark," he corrected with a slight smile. "It's still Mark. So, you saw the money you hoped to get from me as a way out of the life you'd built for yourself?"

"That's the long and the short of it."

"Yet you'd been here for a few hours—sitting right there, across the hall, sharing a drink with me—before that scoundrel showed his face here. And you never mentioned a reward. I'd intended to offer one, but you didn't bring it up. Why is that?"

Jed swallowed. The man had him at a loss. Why hadn't he? That was the entire point, was it not? Collecting money so that he might see his dream come true.

Except...

There was another dream. One he hadn't known his heart possessed until she came into his life. She was the dream he truly wanted, much more than a ranch or any property at all. Just her. He'd build her a castle if she wanted, but it would only matter to him so long as she was happy.

And without her, a ranch simply would not fill the hole she'd left behind. There would no longer be a reason to work toward anything if he wasn't working for something with her. Something they could build together.

"I don't know," was all he could manage to say.

Mark held up his glass, staring at what was left inside. "You care for her a great deal. That much is obvious."

"I would never stand in your way. She came out here to marry you, and you spent the money to bring her here. She deserves a decent man such as yourself, and I'm sure she would make you a good wife."

"Yes. But would she want to?" He looked at Jed. "You didn't deny caring for her."

"No. Why should I? You've seen it for yourself. Lying would be foolish."

"I appreciate your candor." Mark put the glass aside, stood up. "Though I'm sorry to say you've put me in an awkward spot. Because it would appear that the lady cares for you, as well. I thought I saw it in her face back in town, when I met you. She had a sort of shining look whenever she looked at you. I can't explain it well," he muttered, turning away to look out the window.

"As I said, that doesn't matter. You brought her here."

"No. You brought her here, and I understand why you did and why she behaved as she did. How she never killed him herself is beyond me. Surely, she had to protect the child. She was more than likely right when she said he might have killed the babe before it was born."

Jed wished it were possible for a man to die more than once, for he would've relished taking a turn with John Carter.

"I assume she told you of him before you arrived, then?"

"She did," Jed replied, "though I feel she may not have been quite candid enough."

"Well, these aren't things people enjoy describing," Mark murmured. He clasped his hands behind his back, his shoulders rising as he drew in a deep breath. "I've come to a decision."

Jed's heart all but stopped completely.

"If you vow to go straight, that you will never again engage in the sort of activity that brought you here, I'd be glad to have you join my ranch as a hand. I'll be needing a new foreman, but I'd have to give you a trial, first."

Jed lowered the glass onto a side table for fear of dropping it. "You don't mean it."

"I always mean what I say. Do you want the lady?"

"I do."

"And I want her to have a decent life. She deserves that,

as does her child. If you'll care for and provide for both of them, and keep that vow you just made to me, I see no reason why you can't put everything you've learned about ranching into practice here."

Jed was speechless.

Mark turned to him. "What do you say?"

"I'd say you have a deal." The two men clasped hands, smiling over their agreement.

23

No matter how long she stayed in bed, eyes closed, there was no forgetting what she'd seen. John. Dead on the floor.

He was gone. He could hurt her no longer. Her scalp stung as one final reminder of the pain he'd caused—that and the bruise along the side of her face.

Doctor Perkins was a kind man, sweet and patient, and his examination had calmed her fears. "You appear to be just fine," he'd assured her with a warm smile. "You're a strong young woman, and healthy. If your baby made it through the ride you took to get here, it'll make it through anything."

She'd almost forgotten how everyone knew her business. She supposed as the wife of the most successful rancher in the state, it would be something to expect as time went on. Word traveled fast.

"If he still wants me," she whispered with no one but

the wood-paneled walls to hear, alone again. "If he still wants me."

There was no telling now that all was said and done. He'd killed John to protect her, but Mark seemed the type of man who would do the same for any woman in danger. It was, in essence, the same as having killed a rabid dog, to prevent that dog causing harm to others.

If any man could be compared to a rabid dog, it would be John Carter.

This did not mean that Mark had any intention of marrying her. Why would he, knowing how she'd deceived him? She'd intended to lie about the baby and give it his name without his being aware.

What sort of man could forgive that and still marry the woman in question?

Her child would be a bastard, after all. A nameless, fatherless waif. There was no hope of her maintaining privacy in Carson City once word spread of her true identity and that of her child. She could not pretend to be someone she wasn't, that the child's father had been anyone but the brute he was.

The fact that she'd had a husband at all made her a widow, which at least was respectable and might mean a respectable life for her child.

But she'd lied about that husband. She'd come to Nevada in hopes of marrying a second man—no matter the sort of man he was or her reasons for doing it, she'd committed a terrible sin by lying, and her child would carry the mark of that sin.

She'd ruined everything for both of them, when all she'd wanted was a fresh start.

Tears streamed down the sides of her face, soaking into her hair and the feather pillow behind her head. There was no way out now. John might be dead, but he'd managed to destroy her chance at security and happiness just the same. Why couldn't he have let her go? Why couldn't he have gotten himself shot back in Boston?

He didn't even have the decency to do that much.

There was a knock at the door. "Can I come in?" Mark asked.

"Of course." She wiped her eyes before pushing herself up to a sitting position.

"Please, don't feel as though you need to sit up on my account," he implored her as he entered. "I just spoke with the doctor, and he told me you're looking fine. I'm greatly relieved."

"As am I," she breathed, and they both chuckled.

He lingered near the door. "I believe we have a few things to discuss. Wouldn't you agree?"

She'd been waiting for this. The man was due the chance to tell her off for being nothing but a liar, the sort of low woman who would use an innocent man as she'd planned to do to him.

Whatever he said, whatever he threatened, it was no less than what she deserved.

"Yes. We ought to talk." She folded her hands in her lap, steeling herself for what was to come.

"You don't need to look so scared," he smiled.

"Do I look afraid?"

"Like you're trying not to be, yes." He nodded to the bed, a question in his raised brows, and she motioned for him to join her. He perched himself at the foot of the soft mattress, far enough away to remain respectful.

Oh, the entire plan had been a mistake from the start.

He cleared his throat. "You were untruthful, and you took the tickets I provided under false pretenses." His voice was gentle but not entirely forgiving.

Still, it was better than she'd expected. "Yes. I did."

He heaved a deep sigh. "I understand why you did, naturally. I might easily have done the same in your position. I do wish it hadn't been me you chose to deceive."

"I'm sorry. I truly am. You are a good man. You deserve better."

"Thank you for saying that." He cocked an eyebrow. "You also went along with Jed's deception, which bothers me more. You could've told me the truth about him when you got here. Defending him didn't make you seem more... I don't know, legitimate. Why did you lie about him?"

She swallowed and wished there was water nearby. It would provide a way to stall, too.

Why had she lied? When put that way, the story she presented about Jed was beyond understanding. He'd seen the way John treated her with his own eyes and might forgive her desperation to escape that tyranny, but Jed?

That was far less forgivable.

"I... I don't know... He was kind to me..."

"Kidnapping is kindness? I was unaware."

She stared at the delicate lace sewn onto the bedspread. "After that. He was kind to me. He wasn't like the others, the ones who helped him with the robbery. He wanted to quit robbing, and the money would help him do that."

"But why did you care whether he quit robbing people? What did it matter to you? You understand, don't you, how strange this seems?"

"I do, and I wish I could understand it myself," she groaned, her misery growing.

"Melissa. Look at me, please."

It took a moment for her to screw up the courage to lift her eyes from the bedspread and find his. When she did, she found a hint of humor twinkling there.

"I know why you did it, and I think you do, too." He got up, walked to the head of the bed. "I want to tell you this; I release you from our engagement."

Her heart sank like a pebble tossed into a stream. "I knew you would. I just never thought you would be this kind about it."

He chuckled. "Yes, well, I suppose I'm in a kind mood today. You were in an awful spot, and you did what you felt you had to do. I'm only sorry you had to go to such lengths. Knowing what I do now, I can't possibly marry you."

"You're an upstanding man with a good reputation. You could never make me your wife after what I've done. I respect that."

He tilted his head. "Oh, this has nothing to do with my reputation. The fact is, if you were free to be my wife, I would take you in a minute."

She leaned away, this admission the last thing she'd expected. "You mean it?"

"Wholeheartedly. I would call this a rocky start but would gladly accept you as my wife. You would make a good one, I suspect, given the opportunity. And I would see to it that you had that opportunity. I'm sure we could have made a happy life together. Perhaps we might even have come to care a great deal for each other. I would've done my damnedest to make it so, at least."

"What—might I ask what's stopping you?"

He laughed. "You look almost outraged."

"Perhaps not outraged but confused. Wondering why I am not good enough to marry."

"As I said, I would if you were free to be my wife. But you aren't."

She gulped. "Please don't tell me John is still alive."

"Hardly," was his dry reply. "I wasn't referring to that pitiful creature."

"To what did you refer?"

He was infuriating, the way he danced around a subject rather than getting to the heart of the matter.

His response made things no clearer.

He backed away from the bed. "I suspect you'll understand if you give it a bit more thought. When you're feeling up to it, there's somebody downstairs who needs a word with you."

She opened her mouth to ask just what he was getting at, but he'd already left the room. He might have saved her life and forgiven her, but he wore on her nerves more than a little.

There was nothing to do but go downstairs and see what he meant. Passing by the looking glass over the wash basin was unpleasant—her cheek was turning a deep shade of purple. John always could swing hard.

She closed her eyes. He couldn't hurt her anymore. The idea was foreign enough to sound ridiculous, but she had to keep reminding herself until it sank in. He could never hurt her again—and so he deserved no more of her thoughts.

When the baby was born, well, that was another story. The child would always be his. Oh, if only she bore a little girl who favored her mother in coloring.

"I will love you, no matter what," she whispered, hands on her belly. The thought that seeing John and being attacked by him might have brought harm to the baby—she'd heard of women losing pregnancies over much less—had brought home, really and truly, what the child meant to her.

The world. Nothing less.

Downstairs was silent, at least in the front of the house. The study was empty, free of the dead body which had lain there when Melissa climbed the stairs. The doctor had taken him away. There wasn't even any blood on the floor.

Even so, she had no wish to spend more time in that room.

She turned, finding the door to the drawing room open, and crossed the hall to step inside. It was a beautiful room, the wallpaper printed with rows of flowers, the curtains white and gauzy, billowing in the breeze.

She might have entertained guests in this room. Played cards with the ladies at the round table in one corner. Learned to play the shining piano in another corner. Learned the art of conversation and used it while seated around the fire after a long, enjoyable supper.

In front of the fireplace, with its intricate mantle, stood Jed.

"How are you holdin' up?" he asked, his eyes immediately going to her bruised cheek. His jaw tightened.

"Better than I look. Truly."

"Here. Sit down." He gestured to one of the padded chairs nearest the hearth, stepping back when she obliged.

"Mark said somebody down here wanted to speak with me. Was it you?"

He nodded, his hands flexing and relaxing. When he caught her looking at them, he grinned. "My hat's upstairs." Yes, he did have a habit of playing with his hat when there was something difficult to say.

"Just come out with it, then. You know you can talk to me. I'll listen."

He sighed. "This isn't like anything else I'd said before. In fact, I've never spoken these words up until now. Not to anybody. Ever."

She frowned. "What is it? Mark isn't pressing charges against you for kidnapping me, is he?"

He burst out laughing. "Is that what you think this is about? No, the man's the most understanding, generous fella who ever existed. Until meeting him, I couldn't say I was ever embarrassed by another man's generosity, but here we are. We talked about things over a drink and came to an agreement."

"What's that?"

A shy smile crept across his lips. "He's going to give me a chance to be his overseer." The throb of hope in his voice told her he didn't quite believe it yet himself.

It was the second time that day that she'd been struck dumb by something completely unexpected. Words would not form when she moved her mouth.

Jed crouched before her. "Are you all right? You look distressed."

"I—I'm surprised!" She beamed. "If this is what you want, I'm so glad for you! But how did you come about discussing it? And I thought you wanted to buy land for yourself!"

"One thing at a time," he chuckled. "First, it is what I want. Second, we had already talked about ranching and my experience with it before... that." He gestured toward the study, meaning John's appearance and death, which had taken the day and sent it hurtling in another direction. "Third. That part isn't so easy to explain."

"Try."

"So demanding," he whispered with a hint of a smile. "I wanted land of my own, it's true. That was the reason I got myself into this whole mess in the first place. I saw you, heard your name—what the men on the coach thought was your name—and put it all together. I would use you to get money from somebody I knew ran a big ranch."

"I know all of this already."

He went on as though she hadn't said a word. "But here's the surprising thing; that isn't what I want anymore."

"You mean you're just going to give up on your dream?" For some reason, the idea crushed her. "Oh, Jed. I wanted it so much for you, too."

"You did?"

She nodded. "I'm sorry. If you're happy, I'm happy for you. I'm glad you'll be able to settle down now. I just wish it had been the way you hoped."

His shoulders lifted. "Sometimes, we hope for something because we don't know there's anything better out there—and if we know about it, we sure as hell don't think it's meant for us."

"What does that mean?" And why was he looking so deeply into her eyes? Why was he taking her hand? She hardly minded. In fact, she adored every second of it, but that didn't mean it made the first bit of sense.

He drew a deep breath. "Melissa, I want you. You're the dream I want to see come true now. A life with you. If that means promising I'll go straight and working as another man's foreman, that's what I'll do. Because it means I'll be able to take care of you and our family. If that's what you want, too."

She forgot how to breathe. The muscles of her face went slack as she tried to understand what he said over the blissful, ecstatic screaming in her head.

"Melissa?" Oh, the hope in his eyes. The sort of hope she had always wanted to see in a man's eyes, but especially in his.

It was as if she stepped outside herself and was watching over her own shoulder. Her hands in his, resting on her lap. His tense, anxious pose, every muscle tightened as he knelt in front of her. The hardening of his jaw when she didn't answer.

Not that she didn't want to. She simply couldn't speak over the pressure in her chest, over the heart which had suddenly jumped into her throat.

She knew too well what he meant about not knowing a dream was meant for her. Because until that very day, the most she'd ever hoped for was to marry a kind man who would believe her child was his own. She did expect to love her husband or even for him to love her. She could only hope he would be gentler than the men she'd known throughout her life.

It was the best she'd dared hope for.

Until that very moment, in the drawing room, with her hands in Jed's.

"Did... did you ask me something?" she breathed.

"Not exactly, but I will now." He cleared his throat. "Melissa, will you be my wife?"

"Oh, yes." She withdrew her hands so she might throw her arms around his neck, all but crushing him to her. The only thing she could seem to do was laugh with joy—there had to be a way to vent it, after all, or else she might burst.

He laughed with her, both of them sounding surprised and thrilled and a little overwhelmed.

"You mean it?" he asked on pulling away. A shadow of doubt crossed his face. "You aren't just saying yes because you need a husband?"

"Jed." She took his face in her hands, suddenly very grave. "I've been wishing for days that I wasn't promised to another man, that the two of us might be together. I didn't think you wanted me."

"I was sure you could never want me, being who I am."

"Who you were," she corrected. "And that isn't really who you were. It was what you did, that's all." One of her hands dropped to his chest. "This is who you are. And I love who you are."

He took her hand, kissed it. "Bless you. I don't know what I did to earn a woman like you, but I'll be damned if I don't do everything in my power to keep you."

"Even..." She touched her belly, which would soon grow larger. A reminder of a child that wasn't his.

He placed his hand over hers. "This baby is yours and mine. It'll have my name, and I'll love it like my own. I promise you that."

He caught her lips with his own before she dissolved into tears, kissing her in spite of the dampness on her cheeks. This time, she could kiss him with the fullness of her heart, without hesitation or the sense of something illicit sparking between them.

While illicitness had its place, this was far nicer. Knowing his would be the only lips she would ever kiss again, that he would be the only man to make her heart take off at a wild speed, to make her pulse race and blood rush in her ears loud enough to drown out all other sounds.

That she could take the rest of her life to memorize the taste of him, the smell of leather on his clothing, on his skin. Part of him.

That it would be his warm, knowing hands on her body, pressing into her flesh with growing need.

That it would be his heart against hers, beating at the same frantic pace. That strong, good, noble heart she'd loved for longer than she realized at the time.

The heart that she would do everything in her power to keep safe, until the end of her days.

EPILOGUE

Mark raised his glass of ruby red wine. "While this is not the toast I'd planned to make this evening, I'm glad to make it nonetheless. I look forward to a new chapter in the history of Furnish Ranch with Jed as my foreman, and Melissa to keep us all in line."

He dropped a friendly wink her way, earning a grin from her.

"I don't know if there are enough hours in the day to keep all your men in line, but I'll do my best until somebody else comes along." And she hoped someone would, as Mark was still in need of a wife. The sense that she'd ruined his chances hung about the edges of her happiness, tainting it a little, but he'd already assured her of his peace with the situation.

This was supposed to be the welcome supper, the one

preceding their wedding the following day. Instead, Mark held it in honor of the wedding of Jed and Melissa, and at the long table sat many of the men with whom Jed would work.

He was in his element, that much was clear, and her heart swelled with pride and gladness for him. This was where he was meant to be, the subject he was most passionate about. Talking about bloodlines and feeding and even such unseemly topics as the mating of steer and cow, topics even Melissa had never heard discussed at the table.

They could have been discussing just about anything and she wouldn't have minded, just for the pleasure of watching Jed light up as he did.

He would be her husband, and they would live in the little house she'd admired upon reaching the ranch that morning. Was it really only that very morning that they'd arrived? Then, she'd been promised to Mark while married to John. Guilty, miserable, wishing it could all be different.

Now, she would not have traded places with any other woman for all the world.

And she would learn about ranching, because she wanted him to be able to come to her at the end of a long day and know she would understand. She wanted to be everything to him, to shower him with all the love she'd never been able to express. A whole lifetime's worth of it, bottled up inside her.

When the baby came—their baby—she would love it

just the same way, for she knew the pain of an unloved child. Hers would never know that feeling.

It would have two parents who loved it very much, who would perhaps spoil it a little and perhaps coax more than a few tears when it came time for discipline, but she'd do everything in her power to make sure they knew how loved they were through it all.

Could it be she'd ever dreaded having this baby?

Because now, she could hardly wait until they were properly introduced.

IT WAS A BEAUTIFUL MORNING, clear and sparkling. Or perhaps that was simply how she saw things, it being such a special day and all.

She did not own a proper wedding dress and had refused up and down when Mark offered to purchase one for her. "You've done more than enough, Mark Furnish, and I refuse to allow you to spend one more cent on me!"

"Jed's already made an arrangement with me over reimbursement for your tickets," he'd argued.

"You men and your arrangements," she'd scoffed. "Women have pride too, you know, and I have just a bit too much of it to allow you to be that generous. You've already released me from our engagement, given Jed a job, offered to hold the wedding here with the same preacher who was supposed to perform ours, you saved me from John..."

He'd held up a hand, the corners of his lips twitching. "Enough. I see your point."

She'd put her hands on her hips. "Are you sure? Because I wasn't finished."

He'd been sure, and so she was about to be wed in the same worn-out calico dress in which she'd arrived at the ranch, carrying an armful of wildflowers. It was tight, to be sure, but the thought of wedding her love while wearing his clothing did not sit right.

Not that it mattered very much. Her bouquet might as well have been the lushest of roses, her dress a gown of silk and lace, jewels at her ears and throat. She might have been wearing a diamond crown. It certainly felt as though she was when she walked across the drawing room on Mark's arm, to where Jed and the preacher waited for her.

She would have wagered good money that the ranch hands had not expected to attend this ceremony, but Jed had insisted they take a short break from work to act as witnesses. A group of men holding their hats in their work-gloved hands, all of them a bit bewildered, a bit embarrassed to witness something so personal, but respectful just the same.

There he was. So handsome. He could have been wearing the most elegant suit, and he could not have looked better to her than he did then, smiling from ear to ear. How had she ever made herself believe she hated him? A lifetime might as well have passed since those first few rough days together.

A lifetime had passed. She'd gone from a frightened girl convinced she could only ever enjoy the very barest of scraps life spared her to a woman certain of herself, her future, her love.

The bespectacled preacher walked them through the vows—she had recited them once before, hadn't she? But they had meant nothing. She hadn't felt them. She'd only felt an empty stomach and relief that it would no longer be empty.

What a child she had been. A poor, lonely child.

Now, there was so much more she wished to promise Jed than a few words, and the warmth in his eyes told her he felt the same. Eyes she hoped would always radiate the love and hope she saw in them just then.

She would love him until the day she died.

And she would know joy and pride, hope and dreaming. There would be tough times and tears—every life had them—but the sweetness of laying her head to rest every night beside that of the man who loved her through it all would temper the sourness and give her the strength to wake up every morning intent on loving him and allowing him to love her.

Looking at him as the preacher blessed their marriage, it was hard to believe there was a time when she thought happiness was out of her reach. That blessings were for other people, not for her. People who could afford the luxury of loving.

"I declare that they are man and wife."

She was the sort of person who could afford to love. Who could be somebody's happy, beloved wife.

Starting right now, the moment her husband sealed their union with a kiss, and for the rest of her life.

KEEP READING for an excerpt from the next *Westward Hearts story!*

EXCERPT

Upper crust classy saloon girl crossed with shrew's temper and sass. Just what a rancher ordered. Actually, no.

Rancher Mark Furnish is in a bind. His ranch is losing money, the banks have turned him down, and his wealthy grandfather back east is refusing to fund the venture anymore unless Mark has a wife. The mail order bride that was supposed to be his has now become his foreman's wife. Time's tight and Mark doesn't have a second to waste. As if that's not bad enough, he doesn't even want to be married to begin with.

The mail order bride thing didn't work out so well for this sexy cowboy rancher. Who says the second time will be a success?

He steps into the saloon for a couple of shots of cure-all and instead discovers a saloon girl that's more like a fiery temple virgin. She refuses all the men's efforts at flirtation and offers to go upstairs for a tryst. This woman's got upper crust class and a shrew's temper.

Maybe he shouldn't have tried to help her. Maybe he wouldn't have been kicked out of the saloon and she wouldn't have been fired. Now she's his responsibility.

This new turn of events is giving his ideas. Why can't he get the words fake wife out of his mind?

CHAPTER 1

Mark Furnish sat atop his favorite horse, a black colt he'd named Star on account of the white star between its eyes which stood out so clean and bright against the silky black coat.

From this vantage point, the Furnish Ranch stretched out before him for thousands of acres in all directions. To the west was the Carson Range, to the east was the long, wide expanse of land which sat between his home and Carson City. A great deal of it was land belonging to the ranch. In fact, while he could not be absolutely certain, he would have bet most of what was visible to him on that clear morning was, indeed, his.

In moments such as this, with the sun rising over the tops of the distant mountains and painting the sky in hues he was certain no artist could ever recreate on canvas, Mark's heart swelled with pride he could not put to words.

Golden sunlight revealed the land by inches, reminding

him of everything his father had worked for. Everything that was his to hold onto and grow, to pass onto his son.

If only he could hold onto it.

Pride soured, leaving a bitter taste in his mouth.

That taste tinged the beauty of what stretched before him. He could no longer lose himself in reverie when he spied a flock of ducks taking wing after washing themselves in the river. No more did the sight of the faithful, frolicking collie dog who ran alongside the hands and their horses make him smile. That dog was just as hard a worker as any man on the place, himself included.

What were they working for?

That was the question which kept him awake nights. It had for months, since long before the arrival of the woman who would indirectly gain him a future foreman.

And make a murderer out of him.

It was not the killing of John Carter which weighed on Mark. He had not given the man much more than a moment's thought after the conclusion of an inquest which had lasted all of an hour, if that. Once the judge had seen the damage John did to Melissa's face and heard the sworn testimony of himself, the hands who were present at the time, and that of Jed Cunningham, the matter was closed.

John Carter had been nothing more than a dog who'd needed putting down.

That was not why Melissa's arrival had been fortuitous, however.

It was the fact that she had not been his to claim for a wife.

She'd already been in love with Jed, and he with her. While Mark needed a wife, badly, he'd not been able to stand in the way of two people longing to be together.

With a sigh, he pressed his heels to Star's ribs, signaling him to move on. There was much to be done, and no time to be spent admiring a sunrise which had come and gone.

The wind picked up as he rode through the grass, one eye keeping watch for the holes left by cursed prairie dogs. The devils. They'd lost one of the horses only a week earlier, its leg badly broken after one hoof slipped into a blasted hole. There'd been no saving the poor beast.

Mark hated waste, especially the waste of a beautiful and rather expensive animal. It was one thing a ranch did not need.

Especially a ranch losing money the way this one was. It reminded him at times of a sack of grain slit with a sharp knife.

He was watching money flow from his ranch like grain from an open sack.

The drought. The sickness that followed. The loss of so many precious heads of cattle, cattle he'd branded and fed and helped round up alongside the ranch hands. Cattle who represented piles of money. Each of them was a pile of money on four legs.

Money he'd lost.

And now, there was nothing to make up for it.

His hands tightened around the reins.

Mark considered himself an intelligent man. A good businessman, his father had always claimed him the better

of them, and he'd been the one to turn a modest purchase
of land and a few hundred head into the thriving enterprise
he'd left upon his untimely death.

When he was a boy, Mark never understood why his
father was so often wound up. Anxious. Easily angered.

His mother had often made up excuses in her gentle
way. He was worried about his work. Tired from working so
hard. Work, work, work. The ranch had come first from the
day they'd arrived until the day the man died of a brain
hemorrhage which Doc Perkins had attributed to overwork
and tension.

Mark had not needed his mother's excuses by then.
He'd been a grown man the day his father slumped over
behind his desk and died on the spot.

Besides, Mother had been gone for two years by the
time that day arrived, her grave long since filled, the grass
growing over her.

Grandfather Calvin had not come out for her funeral
and had certainly not come out for that of the son-in-law
he'd hated since the day he'd announced having purchased
the ranch. There had been no forgiveness, not even in the
light of shared grief after Isabelle Reynolds Furnish's death.

If anything, her death was just one more thing to blame
on her husband, Grandfather Calvin's son-in-law.

Mark's bitter laughter faded in the wind, reaching no
one's ears but his and Star's. To think, the man who'd
reviled the purchase of the ranch was the only one who
could save it.

If the Good Lord had a sense of humor, the one upstairs

was surely getting quite a bit of amusement out of Mark Furnish and his ranch.

He kept the failings of the ranch away from the hands. They didn't need to know how dire the situation might become unless every option had been explored and come up short.

The bank had come up short, that was for sure. Bile rose in Mark's throat whenever he remembered smug Mr. Bernstein in his little office, looking over the ranch's figures and announcing what a bad investment it had suddenly become.

A bad investment? When Mark himself had invested in the town more times than he could remember? When his ranch and the money coming from it had built the very roof over their heads as they sat in that smoke-filled office?

So much for investing in one's home. The minute he'd gone to them for help, they'd turned him away. Even though he owned the ranch free and clear.

"How's it coming along here?" he asked, riding up alongside a group of men inspecting the fencing along the eastern border. "Don't forget to look out for those damned holes."

"Found two today, filled 'em in, but you know what good that'll do." One of the men spat a mouthful of tobacco juice on the ground. Mark would never begrudge the men their habits, Lord knew he had some of his own, but he did thank his lucky stars he'd never picked up the chewing of tobacco.

Smoking was another story.

"I'd love to blast the lot of 'em off the face of the Earth," Mark muttered, eyes sweeping the wide, flat land around them. "How's the fence looking? No cutting or tampering?"

"None that we've seen so far."

That was a relief. The last thing he needed with the state the ranch was in was for angry, resentful neighbors to slice through his fencing in order to water their livestock.

"Thank you," he said with a smile and a tip of his hat. He believed in always thanking the men, making sure they knew how he appreciated them.

That might be all they'd have to take away from their time at the ranch once he was forced to sell.

No wonder his father had died, and no wonder he'd died how he had. Did he carry these burdens on his shoulders? Did he secretly struggle as his son was now struggling?

Why hadn't he ever told Mark how to handle such pressure? Because he'd never been good at handling it himself, and therefore had no advice to give?

To the north of where he sat astride Star was the house. His house. How he'd labored over it, if not with his hands, with his mind. How he'd second-guessed every decision, down to the color of the horsehair sofa and chairs in the drawing room and the pattern on the as-yet-unused china.

Lena had helped, on the days when she could spare time away from her own home roughly twenty miles from his. There was a time when he'd imagined her to be the future lady of Furnish Ranch, and there had been a certain poetry in her being the one to instruct him on what his future wife might enjoy if and when she walked into his life.

It was for the best that nothing had ever solidified between them, just as he knew it was for the best that Melissa had married Jed and not him.

While he needed a wife most desperately now, he would not have trapped her for the world. No matter what was at stake.

How could he have lived with himself in the years thereafter?

Though it would have made a nice touch for his wife to be with child when his grandfather came for a visit. The perfect excuse to throw himself on the old man's mercy. *Please, help me maintain this as a legacy for my unborn child. Make it possible for us to avoid destitution.*

It was not meant to be.

Something better was meant to be. It had to be.

What else did he have to hang on to otherwise?

He continued the ride to the house, its four floors looming larger the closer he drew. How he'd imagined his mail-order bride enjoying the sunsets with him from the porch which wrapped around the entire first floor. Granted, he was rarely available to enjoy a sunset, but he could still dream of a time when he would be.

How he'd imagined her tending his mother's rose garden which Cook, his only live-in household servant, currently took care of. Lena and her brother, Ryan, lent out their girls once a week to do the dusting and changing of linens, the laundering of his clothing. As he lived alone and kept most of the upstairs rooms closed up, there wasn't much to be done.

It ought to be a wife overseeing these tasks and so many more. He knew this, but that didn't mean the knowing of it had to give him any pleasure.

The entire fiasco with Melissa had been ill-fated from the start. The pressure to look for a wife had led him to take desperate measures. Were it up to him alone, he never would have considered looking for a bride, especially not one he'd found through an ad in the newspapers up and down the East coast.

He'd thought that a touch of genius on his part. His grandfather would've liked to know Mark had married a girl from his side of the country. The fact that Melissa had hailed from Boston would've made it perfect. The Reynolds family was originally from Philadelphia, where Calvin still lived and served on his bank's board of directors.

The same bank where he'd arranged a place for his son-in-law, Mark's father, albeit in the St. Louis branch.

Another slight. Calvin had taken it personally when Paul Furnish walked out of the job he'd secured for him.

"What a mess," Mark muttered, shaking his head at the foolishness of it all. Not being able to freely reach out to his grandfather as a grandson ought to, all thanks to the old man's pride and bad blood which had nothing to do with Mark.

Cook was finishing up cleaning what the men had left behind after a hasty breakfast. He fixed himself a cold plate of bacon and biscuits and a cup of hot, strong coffee which likely would've stripped the varnish from the floor.

It was time to retire to his study and pore over the books one more time.

As though that would be of any help.

I hope you enjoyed
A Highwayman's Mail Order Bride!
Next in the series...
A Rancher's Pretend Mail Order Bride!

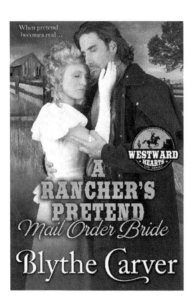

Sign up for the newsletter to be notified of new releases.

Click on link for
Newsletter
or put this in your browser window:

landing.mailerlite.com/webforms/landing/p6l2s1

35369799R00146